D0149078

VICIOUS

VICIOUS

a novel

JEFF GOMEZ

Harrow Books

"My week beats your year."

—*Lou Reed*

MONDAY

VELVET TRIM ON a gold-and-black jacket catches his eye and he stops typing.

"Don't stare, Lou, it's not polite."

He grins like a schoolboy and looks away. Vera drops a stack of mail and pushes the silver cart to the next desk, delivering a handful of files. It's early. The office is still waking up. People talk and sip coffee from Styrofoam cups. A few are munching on pastries and donuts from the Grove Bakery. Lou can smell almond from a bear claw. His dad's in his office at the far end of the long space, beyond the dozen gray steel desks, rows of beige filing cabinets, and the small reception area near the front door.

Lou, sitting up and craning his head, can see the back of his father's dark-brown leather chair. It's turned toward the wall, a coiled black cord extending to a phone on the desk Lou can't see but knows is there. Sidney Reed is small, so all Lou can see is the chair. Above the hum of all the conversations, and even the traffic outside, Lou can hear his father's voice somberly discussing facts and figures. Taxes. Everyone else is wasting time and catching up from the weekend, but not his dad.

Lou watches as Vera parks her cart and begins talking

to a group of older secretaries a few desks over while Ray, the office boy, sits with his feet up and reads the latest issue of *Hot Rod*. The secretaries are all smiling and nodding, even though Lou knows none of them particularly like Vera. They think she's low-class because she lives in the Bronx and dresses badly. But if it means they don't have to do their work, they'll listen to anybody.

After working there for almost a month, Lou has learned the various rhythms of the office and the people who work there. He knows which days will be busy, which ones are always light, and what hours see the most activity. He notices when people arrive and when they leave. Most days, they all order in sandwiches from the luncheonette down the street. Vera has egg salad, Audrey and Moira eat either tuna fish or tomato sandwiches, and Ray orders a burger and a malt, like the teenager he still is. Lou observes all this as if he were watching a TV show. A boring TV show.

He reaches for the stack of mail. It's small for a Monday. With a heavy silver letter opener, he slices the tops of envelopes, glances at the contents, and separates the correspondence into piles. Checks, bills, letters from clients. Flyers and junk mail go right into the trash. By now, Vera's moved on with her cart, people are sitting at their desks, and the office begins to generate its usual low purr of ringing phones, people typing, filing cabinets opening and closing.

The firm handles mainly businesses and estates. New accounts come by word of mouth, and most matters are taken care of over the phone or by letter. Not many clients come to visit or for meetings. Instead, Lou's dad likes to go to them. He thinks visiting clients at their home or office is the personal touch that sets him apart from other accountants.

Lou grabs the separated stacks of mail and walks around the office, delivering the piles to various employees. Audrey takes a first look at any correspondence from clients, Jeanie collects the checks and enters them into the ledger before they're deposited, and the firm's general manager—Sheldon Mayer—pays the bills. Letters addressed to Sidney Reed are left in a tray outside his office. The tray is empty, but another one next to this holds handwritten responses from his father or a secretary. This is what Lou has to type up and send out, five days a week. He picks up three outgoing letters and walks back to his desk.

He's worked in the office on and off since high school, coming in over the years to occasionally run errands or do what he's doing now, typing letters. He always made sure to not stay for long. It's the end of September, and he's been here ever since he quit his band the week before Labor Day. It's the longest he's ever worked for his dad. Lou had been offered a job at the firm in '64, right after he graduated from college, but he turned it down. Lou didn't want to be just a bookkeeper. Didn't want to be like his old man.

He sits down and turns to the typewriter, a blue IBM. Unlike the cheap manuals he had during his college years at Syracuse, the IBM is electric. The lightest touch on the keys will make it strike. He types a few lines, keeping his eyes on the memo Moira had written by hand.

"Where'd you learn how to do that?"

Lou looks up. Ray's standing there. The magazine he'd been reading is now tucked under his left arm. Lou tilts his head and can read *BUGGIES—New Generation of Street Roadsters.*

"Do what?"

"Type with all your fingers like that."

Lou looks down. Both hands are hovering above the keyboard. The fingers on his left hand are poised over A, S, D, and F while his right hand rests on top of J, K, L, and the semicolon. Each of his thumbs are in place to hit the space bar.

"Took typing in high school."

"Why?"

"Was my mom's idea. 'Always have something to fall back on'—that's what she used to say. She was a secretary herself, you know."

Ray grins and says, "Nah, didn't know that."

With his thick Brooklyn accent, *that* sounds more like *dat*. Lou had been born and raised in Brooklyn, just like Ray, but he doesn't have much of an accent. Lou and his family moved to Long Island when he was nine. He doesn't have much of a Long Island accent either. The two ways of speaking had sort of cancelled each other out.

"Yup," says Lou, continuing to type, "she was crowned 'Queen of the Stenographers' back in '39."

Ray tries to whistle but it just comes out as air.

"'The typewriter is holy.' You know who said that?"

Ray looks puzzled.

"You did, Lou. Just now."

"Jesus, Ray, I meant who said it *first*."

Ray just shakes his head.

"Allen Ginsberg," Lou answers.

The boy nods, but Lou knows that Ray has no idea who Allen Ginsberg is. No one in the office does. They're all too busy reading *Love Story* or *Jonathan Livingston Seagull.*

Lou doesn't say anything else, he just types the next two lines. Ray keeps standing there.

"Something else I can help you with, Raymond?"

Ray smarts at hearing his proper name. Lou knows just how he feels. Only his parents, and a few of the older employees in the office—the ones who'd been with his dad for years—call him Lewis.

"Mr. Mayer said you could write me a receipt for the stamps I bought last week when I had to run those big packages down to Hempstead. I need that before I can get reimbursed."

"Sure, Ray, I'll get that for you right now."

Ray says thanks and finally moves on. Lou types the last sentence and pulls the paper from the typewriter, the carriage making a zipping sound. He gives Moira's memo a final look and—not finding any errors—moves on to the trio of letters he'd picked up from the tray outside his dad's office. The first one is from Audrey to a new client, requesting the usual paperwork. Typing it only takes a minute. After giving it a quick read, he walks over to Audrey's desk to get her to sign it. A drawer on the left side of her desk is open and Lou can see a small plastic transistor radio. Above all the other noise of the office, he hears the Carpenters. "Close to You." She looks up from her paperwork. She's wearing cat-eye glasses with rhinestones.

"How we doing today, Lou?"

"You know me, Audrey," he replies in an even tone as he hands her the letter, "just happy to be here."

She grins, picks a pen from a mug that says JONES

BEACH, and signs the letter. As he walks away, Lou spots Vera at Moira's desk. She's pulled one of the chairs from the reception area. Moira has one of the firm's ledgers open, and Lou can hear her explaining basic bookkeeping to Vera.

"This is called a trial balance. It's a quick report that lists all the debt and credit balances for every account."

Lou sits back down at his desk. The next letter is from his dad. It's short, just a sentence scrawled on one of the firm's note cards. Lou cocks his head, trying to decipher his father's handwriting. The words are tiny and almost indecipherable. Lou's convinced the other secretaries only like having him around because he's the one person who can read his dad's writing. It takes him a second, but he finally gets it. *This client's taxes are currently under audit and thus cannot be released at this time.*

As Lou reaches for the original letter, which is from a law firm in New York and is signed by a secretary, he discovers the paper is thin and oniony—it's almost see-through. The typed words are faint, more gray than black.

Our firm has become aware that you are in possession of the belongings of Samuel Donato, who died on February 10, 1967. We represent Mr. Donato's only living relative, who wishes to take possession of his cousin's estate. Please confirm at your earliest convenience what you will require to transfer ownership of Mr. Donato's assets.

This is not a typical letter. In all the time he's worked for his father, Lou's never come across anything like this. The firm sometimes handles estate taxes, but they'd never before held on to a deceased person's possessions. Lou reads the letter again, as well as his dad's response. None of it makes any sense. They're asking about the guy's stuff, but his dad's reply is about taxes.

Lou grabs a sheet of office stationery and winds it into the typewriter. He types out the name of the law firm, addresses the letter to the secretary, and begins to compose the body of the letter.

> *Regarding the release of Samuel Donato's possessions, at this time we*

He stops.

Lou gets up and walks over to the long row of filing cabinets that line the back wall of the office. He finds the *D*'s and opens the heavy drawer, flipping through the various files as he searches for *Donato, Samuel*. He finds the file holder, sandwiched between *Aldiss Deans* and *Drapes by Frederick*, but the actual file is missing. There's nothing but an empty space where the file should be. Lou closes the drawer and looks around.

Sheldon Mayer stores the names and addresses of all the firm's current clients on a Rolodex that he keeps on his desk. He's forever referencing and updating it, in case Lou's dad needs a phone number or the address of someone they're doing business with. If Samuel Donato's a client, he'll be in Sheldon's Rolodex.

Lou glances across the room. Sheldon's desk is empty, and he doesn't seem to be in the office. He was there a second ago, concentrating on something through those thick glasses of his, but now he's gone. This means he's either in with Lou's dad or else he stepped out for a moment. As Lou walks to Sheldon's desk, he hears Vera ask Moira, "What's the difference between accounts payable and accounts receivable?" Lou notices that Vera's scribbling down notes in a small notebook. She's wearing peace symbol earrings, and they move back and forth as she writes.

Lou quickly moves behind Sheldon's desk and flips through the Rolodex. There's no Samuel Donato.

"Hey, Lou."

Ray appears out of nowhere. Lou's startled, but doesn't look up. He knows that Sheldon also keeps a roster of ex-clients. This is kept in a small black-and-white notebook. Maybe Donato will be listed there. Lou lifts up various files and folders, looking for the notebook.

"You got that receipt for me?"

"For what, Ray?"

"Last week. Hempstead, I just told you."

Lou shakes his head, as if trying to shake the memory loose.

"Sorry, Ray. Sometimes it's hard for me to remember things."

"Yeah, I know," Ray says. "Because of the . . ."

Lou stands up straight as Ray begins to back away.

"Because of what, Ray?"

In the silence, Lou hears a new song come on Audrey's little radio. "Julie, Do Ya Love Me."

Instead of speaking, Ray just makes a noise like a buzzing bee. Lou knows what he's referring to. Creedmoor.

"I'm sorry, Lou. Didn't mean nothing by it." Ray gestures to the desks, where the secretaries are all poring over paperwork. "Some of the girls, they told me."

"Get out of here, Ray. Go do your job."

Ray backs off and, trying to make himself useful,

begins to take lunch orders even though it isn't even eleven. Some people are still sipping their morning coffee.

Lou has to shut his eyes tight to remember what he's doing at Sheldon Mayer's desk. Then it hits him. Samuel Donato. The notebook of ex-clients. He finally finds it and quickly checks both the *D*'s and the *S*'s. No mention of the dead man there either.

He returns Sheldon's things to the way he'd found them and walks back to his desk. Retrieving the original letter about Donato, and his father's response, he approaches Sidney Reed's office.

The door's open, like usual. Lou gives a quick knock before entering.

"Hey, Pops, I just got this letter."

His dad's looking over a huge ledger. Lou can see the red and black ink. The desk is filled with all kinds of papers: receipts, letters, contracts, more ledgers. An extension attached to the left side of the desk holds a black typewriter, a Selectric, the same as Lou's. On the far corner of the desk is a huge adding machine, its surface a field of numbers in off-white and green. Sidney Reed looks up.

"Good morning, Lewis, what is it?"

Sidney Reed wears a jacket and tie to the office every day, even in the summer. Above his father's wire-framed glasses, his hair is thinning. He looks older than fifty-seven. If Lou looks hard, he can see himself in his father's face. He tries not to look that hard.

"Why do we have some dead guy's stuff? And why don't we just give it back?"

Lou lets go of the letter and his dad's handwritten response. They float down to the desk. His dad picks up the original letter. Not looking up from the paper, he answers, "We don't have a dead man's 'stuff,' Son."

"Yeah, but"—Lou motions toward the letter—"that law firm says—"

"It's not that easy, Lewis. There are . . . complications. It's a special case."

Lou points to the office floor behind them. "I checked the cabinets, and his file seems to be missing. I also didn't find him on Sheldon's Rolodex, or in the notebook of ex-clients."

Sidney Reed smiles slightly, as if impressed by his son's initiative.

"It's a private matter, Lewis." He folds up the letter. "On second thought, I'll handle it myself."

Lou shrugs and turns to leave. Before he steps out of the office, he looks back and sees his dad slip the folded-up letter into a long walnut credenza that lines the back wall. On top of the credenza is a framed photo of Lou and his sister from when they were kids.

Lou walks back to his desk and sits down. He pulls the unfinished letter from the typewriter and places it in the top drawer of his desk, adding it to the assortment of pens, pencils, and loose change. He grabs the letter opener and places it in the drawer too.

Ray floats over, notepad in hand.

"Hey, Lou, I'm getting lunch today from Wetson's. You want anything?"

"No, Ray." He tries to shake the letter about the dead man's things out of his mind, but can't. "I'm good."

•

Sidney Reed appears in front of Lou's desk at five thirty.

"Come on, Son. Time to go home."

Lou doesn't stop typing. He just grunts, "Give me a sec."

His father looks at his watch and proceeds to roll back and forth on the balls of his feet while he waits.

Lou finishes the letter, pulls it from the typewriter, places it on the desk. It's to a client confirming that they've paid their estimated taxes. He'll address the envelope and stick a stamp on it tomorrow. Lou sends out a dozen letters like that a week. He typed up two just today. It's getting to the point where he doesn't even need his dad or one of the secretaries to draft replies to the questions that come into the office. After typing hundreds of letters over the past couple of weeks, Lou's beginning to know how to answer them himself.

He gets up and follows his dad to the door.

The office is nearly deserted. All the secretaries except Audrey have gone home, and the only other person left is Sheldon Mayer. He sits in the far corner, tallying up everyone's hours from the previous week. The first person to leave had been Ray, who was dismissed shortly after four because there was nothing else for him to do. Right after Sheldon released him, Ray got a great big grin and bounded out the door. A few seconds later everyone in the office, not to mention on the entire street, heard him fire up his 1964 Pontiac GTO and speed off.

Sidney Reed says good night to Sheldon and Audrey, and they say good night back. Lou doesn't say anything. Lou and his father walk in silence outside and down the street, rounding the corner and heading for the parking lot located behind the building. Sidney Reed doesn't have a dedicated parking space but, being a creature of habit, he parks every day in the same spot. They approach the white Mercedes.

"Pops, why do you take the nice car and make Mom drive the Lincoln?"

They get in the car. Sidney Reed starts the engine and begins to pull out of the parking lot.

"Well, Lewis, sometimes I travel to meetings and appointments. The Mercedes helps to make a good impression." He pauses as two boys in Cub Scout uniforms cross in front of them. "Besides, your mother enjoys driving the Lincoln."

Lou hits at the burgundy leather interior with his right hand. "You're doing well with your tax business. Buy her a Mercedes too. Don't be so cheap."

Sidney Reed pulls into traffic. As he slowly drives down Main Street, people who know him wave and he waves back. A woman outside Viebrock's gets a big smile when she sees it's Sidney Reed behind the wheel.

"Son, I appreciate your interest in my affairs, and your help at the firm, but I'm not quite ready to take financial advice from you."

He chuckles, but Lou does not.

"Yeah, well," Lou continues, a sneer in his voice, "how would you like to drive around town in some cheap American-made car?"

"I'd like it just fine, Lewis." They pass Betsy's Fashion Fabrics and Pizza D'Amore, the 25¢ SLICE sign blinking in the dusk. "I did it all the time when we lived in Brooklyn."

All of Lou's best memories are from Brooklyn. Ice cream at Al & Shirley's, egg creams from Becky's on Kings

Highway, rooting for the Dodgers. He'd even liked his elementary school, PS 192. There was always something happening in Brooklyn.

Long Island had seemed to Lou in 1953 a wasteland. It was nothing but acres and acres of tract houses. Levittown, the original postwar cookie-cutter suburb, was just ten miles away. Moe Tucker, his former drummer, was from there. It's a place where all the homes look the same. Even the people look the same. And now, seventeen years later, it isn't much better.

The only good thing about Freeport is that he hated it so much it forced him to leave. He moved to New York City as fast as he could. His first apartment was a huge loft with no furniture or heat. He ate nothing but oatmeal because that's all he and his bandmate John Cale could afford. But he preferred that—with all its freedom—to the crushing banality of the suburbs. He hates Long Island, and yet here he is, being driven home by his dad after a day's work. His salary's forty bucks a week. In the Velvet Underground, his manager once got them two grand. What the fuck happened?

They pass Korvettes, the department store where Lou bought his first stereo. He turns and watches as it gets smaller and smaller and then, finally, disappears as his dad turns onto Route 24. It's a fifteen-minute drive from the office in Garden City to the house in Baldwin.

When Sidney Reed turns onto North Brookside, Lou looks at the various houses pass by. There's no distinct style. Some are made out of red brick and have white picket fences, while others are sleek in a way that had once seemed modern but now just seems dated. Each house has a lush green lawn. Tall, leafy oak and plum trees line the sidewalks. The homes sit on large lots, with at least twenty feet between them. In Brooklyn, your neighbors are just a wall away and people are packed into tight spaces that extend into all three dimensions. In Freeport, most houses are just a single story and each block only holds a handful of homes.

Lou had known plenty of kids from these streets. His best friend growing up, Allan Hyman, was just a few blocks away. Terry Lee, Norman Goldstein, and Johnny DeKam—from Freeport High—they all lived around here too. Lou tries to imagine what they're doing now. He wonders whether they moved back to Freeport after college. He slouches low in the seat in case they're around, not wanting to be seen.

Sidney Reed rounds the corner and pulls into the driveway, which is actually on Maxson even though the address is Oakfield Avenue because the house was built on a corner lot. It's one story, with three bedrooms, a sloping roof, and vinyl siding. The family has lived here ever since they moved from Brooklyn.

As they sit and wait for one of the two garage doors to open, a plane flies overhead, having just taken off from JFK. Lou looks up as it passes by, the jets quickly drowned out by the revving of the Mercedes as his dad slowly guides the car into the garage. Lou notices that his mom's black Lincoln barely fits in its space, the chrome grill pushing against cardboard boxes filled with holiday decorations.

Lou jumps out of the car, not waiting for his father. Walking to the door, Lou passes a trio of steel garbage cans and a pair of wooden tennis rackets sitting on a shelf. The garage opens into the kitchen, where his mother's making dinner. His grandmother has recently begun living there as well. She's staying in his sister's old room since she's at college, studying premed. Lou has always loved his sister. Bunny was the only person he missed after moving out. She's planning on coming down for the weekend to have dinner at the club.

His grandmother sits on the couch watching *Hollywood Squares* on a twenty-three-inch Zenith color TV housed in a dark oak frame. Lou looks around for his dog.

"Hey, Ma, where's Seymour?"

"In the backyard," his mom says, stirring something in a pot. "He needs to be walked, so please do that before dinner."

Lou nods and then leans in and kisses his grandmother on the head. He tastes hairspray.

"How ya doing, Bubbie?"

"Well, Lou, well."

She's his mom's mom, Rebecca. She came over from Poland before the war and still hasn't lost the accent. *Well* sounds like *vell*.

His mother, Toby, enters the living room wiping her hands on an apron. Her short hair is turning gray.

"Lewis, where's your father?"

"I left him at the office."

She looks confused until Sidney Reed enters a second later. When he approaches his wife and gives her a kiss, Lou looks away. On the TV, Paul Lynde's in the center square, as usual. Burt Reynolds is in the top right corner, chewing gum and grinning.

His dad disappears to change his clothes. Every night it's the same routine. Come home, *Hollywood Squares*, dinner. You can set your watch by it.

"Lewis, you received a package."

Lou turns to see his mom holding a thin square box. From across the room, he can see the big *A* of the Atlantic Records logo.

"Is this your new album, Lewis? From your group?"

He was trying to forget about that. A few weeks ago, his publicist had sent him a test pressing, and it had made Lou apoplectic. Songs had been edited and the sequence was all out of order. He'd managed to push it out of his mind but now here it is, in the house, five feet away. He can't escape it any longer. And not just that—it's on its way to stores. Reviews will be printed. And yet none of it makes any difference because he quit the band. It doesn't exist anymore. What's inside that box is a ghost.

"Shit."

His grandmother laughs, but his mom scolds him.

"Lewis! I don't want you using that kind of language in my house."

"Jesus, Mom, I'm twenty-eight."

"I don't care how old you are, this is still *my* house."

She walks across the living room and hands him the package. Lou takes it warily. As she returns to the kitchen, his grandmother turns back to the TV. *Plop plop, fizz fizz, oh what a relief it is.*

As Lou stands there holding the package, Sidney Reed reenters the living room. He's still wearing slacks and a dress shirt, but he's taken off his tie and has traded his wing tips for slippers and his blazer for a cardigan. He picks up a copy of the *Long Island Daily Press* that's folded and waiting for him on a light-brown leather recliner.

Figuring he can't put it off any longer, Lou rips off

the tape and opens the package. He pulls out the album. In an arc at the top it says THE VELVET UNDER-GROUND LOADED. Lou rolls his eyes at the garish illustration and quickly turns the sleeve over. Reading the back, he feels his face get hot. His hands begin to shake.

Lou glances at his watch. It's past six. No one will be at Atlantic now, not on a Monday. He quickly goes to his room and fishes out Danny Fields's home number from a notebook. He storms through the living room and grabs the green plastic phone from the wall of the kitchen. His mother's tasting something with a big wooden spoon as Lou dials Danny's number.

While it rings, Lou's father calls out, "It smells great in there, dear!"

More ringing. Lou's mother answers, "Thank you, sweetheart!"

Lou's about to hang up when someone finally picks up, only it's not Danny. It's his answering service.

"Care to leave a message?"

"Yeah," he grunts, "tell him to call Lou Reed at home. It's important. I'm out in Freeport at 378-7548."

He slams the phone into its cradle. The bells inside clang together. Everyone in the house jumps.

"Ma," Lou barks, "pour me a scotch."

TUESDAY

L OU LOOKS AT the office clock. 9:23. It's too early to
call Atlantic. No one will be there, not even the
receptionist. He'd tried Danny Fields three more times
the night before, but never reached him. Lou had consid-
ered going in to Manhattan to try and find him. It's only
a forty-five-minute drive, and Lou knew of half a dozen
places he could have looked for Danny. Dark booths
where they'd spent hours over the years engaging in
intense, amphetamine-fueled discussions. The problem
was, Lou knew everything else he'd find if he couldn't
find his publicist, and he's trying to stay away from all
that. Moving back to Long Island is his chance to recover
and regroup, and one night in Manhattan—even a Monday—could have put an end to it all.

When Lou looks at the clock again—9:27, still too
early—he sees Ray holding court with Vera and some of
the younger secretaries. They all like him and treat him
like a mascot, setting him up on dates with their cousins
(Lou's heard about plenty of first dates, but no second
ones). As Ray struts back and forth telling a story, the
bell-bottoms of his jeans swirl around his platform shoes.

All the girls howl except for Jeanie. She's a recent hire Lou doesn't know very well.

"You're a phony, Ray. You'd never have told him that. Never in a million years."

Ray begins to loudly swear that the story went down just like he told it. This causes Sheldon Mayer to look up from his work, adjust his glasses, clear his throat. Ray and the others notice and quickly hustle to their next tasks. Lou grabs a piece of office stationery and winds it into the typewriter. Turning on the IBM, it slowly purrs to life. He types.

Jeanie was a spoiled young brat
She thought she knew it all

When Vera comes by with the morning mail, Lou's distracted and stops typing. He turns from the typewriter to the mail. He separates the stack of correspondence into their usual piles and delivers them to the appropriate people. Sitting back down, he notices it's 10:02. He picks up the phone and dials. The female voice that answers after two rings is young and chipper.

"Atlantic Records, how can I help you?"

"Yeah, Danny Fields."

She puts the call through. It rings a dozen times before the same voice answers again.

"I'm sorry, he's not picking up. Would you like to leave a message?"

"Tell him Lou Reed called and to call me back. It's, like, an emergency."

After hanging up, he pounds his fist on the keys of the typewriter. A random assortment of jumbled letters strike the page. Grabbing the paper from the typewriter, he reads the lines about Jeanie. He likes them and thinks maybe he can use them somewhere. When he goes to place the sheet in the top drawer of his desk, he sees the abandoned letter from the day before. He pulls it out and reads what he'd typed.

Regarding the release of Samuel Donato's possessions, at this time we

It takes him a second to remember what this is referencing. Then it clicks. The dead man. Lou gets up and walks across the office. His dad's office door is open, but he's not at his desk. Lou approaches Audrey. Her radio is playing a commercial for Goldenberg's Peanut Chews. *Taste that famous tantalizing taste.*

"Hey, Audrey, you see where my dad went?"

Her desk is a mound of papers and receipts. Lou scans the various bits. All he sees are numbers.

"Client meeting. Should be back in a bit." She looks up. "You need him?"

"No, no, was just curious."

She goes back to her work as Lou walks back to his dad's office. He pretends to be interested in the letters that are in the tray outside the open door. His dad's chair is pushed aside, so Lou can clearly see the credenza where Sidney Reed had placed the letter about the dead man the day before. Glancing back toward the main room, everyone seems engrossed in a task. Even Ray is busy restocking a supply cabinet. Lou slips inside his dad's office.

He can't get over how much the room smells like his father. Aftershave. The smell of his dad's suit after he's worn it a couple of times. In the seat of the brown leather chair, he spots white flakes of dandruff.

Turning to the credenza, the framed picture of him and his sister stops him for a moment. In the black-and-white photo, he looks to be about eight or nine, which would make her four or five. She's wearing a gingham summer dress and he's in shorts and a madras shirt. His hair is short, with bangs, as is hers. They're on a lawn somewhere, with big trees and the family car—an old Studebaker—in the background. Lou can't remember the location. It's certainly not where they grew up. No block on Brooklyn looked like that. They must have been visiting someone, a weekend trip to the country. Lou, with his buckteeth, has his arm around his sister.

Opening the credenza, he spots only odds and ends. A few pencils, a stapler, a box of paper clips. Envelopes and note cards with the firm's address. He checks every shelf twice. The letter is gone. So is the file. He turns to the desk and opens and closes various drawers. All he sees are the usual papers. There's nothing about the dead man. No file, no letter.

Lou tries the last drawer. With a strong pull, it opens with a rusty squeak. It's empty except for a lone file sitting at the bottom. Lou reaches for it and places it on his dad's desk. It's a thin manila folder labeled *Donato, Samuel.* Most of the client files hold years of tax returns, correspondence, and stacks of receipts or cancelled checks. They're sometimes as thick as a phone book, held together with giant rubber bands that look like a fan belt, but not this one. It seems to hold no more than a dozen pieces of paper.

Opening the file, the first thing Lou sees is the letter

and his dad's response from the day before. He sets that aside. The next thing he comes across is a bunch of receipts. They're for monthly charges to a storage facility in Manhattan. Lou grabs a few. Each one is for $92.89.

"A hundred bucks," Lou says out loud. "That's a lot."

When he was in college his dad had needed to get a few storage lockers nearby for older files, the stuff no one ever looked at or needed. And even though that space had held dozens upon dozens of wooden crates filled with tens of thousands of pages, the monthly charge had been under fifty dollars. Lou can't imagine the size of a space that would cost twice that. He quickly flips through all the receipts. There are about forty of them, dating back to early 1967. His dad's name is on each one.

The next thing in the file is a small scrap of paper, a clipping from the *New York Times*. It's a story about the death of Samuel Donato, a paragraph from deep inside the paper alongside a small and grainy photo. It says that Samuel Donato, a Vietnam veteran, had been found dead in his apartment on the Upper East Side of Manhattan from a gunshot wound. There's no mention of suspects or even an investigation. Lou can't tell from the scant details if Donato was murdered or committed suicide. Lou examines the picture. Donato seems to be a large man, with broad shoulders and a square jaw. He's wearing a suit and tie, and his fair hair is cut short in a military style.

The final document in the file is an insurance policy. After two pages of what looks to Lou like standard language, there's a long list of the dead man's possessions. This is what the law firm's trying to get back. Scanning the various items, it seems to Lou like what you'd expect. Furniture. Appliances. Clothes. Lou notices that the price for nearly everything is high. The story doesn't mention Donato's age, but Lou figures him to be older, perhaps an officer with a pretty high rank—he's not some grunt who was drafted. Plus, the fact that he lived on the Upper East Side shows he had money. Lou is beginning to see why that long-lost relative wants to get their hands on this stuff.

Lou's about to return the policy to the file when the second-to-last item on the list catches his eye. ORIGINAL PAINTING BY ANDY WARHOL. He runs his finger horizontally over the form to see how much Donato had paid for it. Instead of a number, it says, *Gift of the artist.*

"Can I help you, Lou?"

He looks up and sees Sheldon Mayer standing in the doorway. Sheldon's arms are folded across his chest.

"No, I'm just look—I mean, checking on something."

"In Mr. Reed's office?"

"I'm Mr. Reed too, remember?"

Sheldon's face turns red and his glasses seem to fog. He backs out of the doorway.

Lou looks over the papers quickly one more time, puts everything back into the file, and returns the thin folder to the bottom of the drawer, where he found it. With a shove he gets the drawer closed again. As he leaves his dad's office, Lou refuses to look in Sheldon Mayer's direction.

Back at his desk, Lou tries to put together the pieces. Why would Warhol give a Vietnam vet one of his paintings? And why has his dad been paying for years to store the possessions of a dead man? Lou looks again at the half-completed line from the day before.

Regarding the release of Samuel Donato's possessions, at this time we

His dad's excuse about Donato being audited isn't true. Lou hadn't found any trace of Donato's taxes, or a letter from the IRS about an audit, or anything else. And while Donato's name hadn't meant anything to him, his picture had unsettled something inside Lou. There was a slim twitch of recognition. Had he seen him before? Maybe he was a client, and Lou had met him during one of his infrequent trips to the office over the years, or at their country club during a Saturday night dinner. But if that was the case, why had Warhol given him a painting? Lou could certainly believe Donato was a rich guy his dad had fawned over to win an account, but how did Andy fit into that? Freeport wasn't exactly Warhol's scene.

Lou grabs a light-blue denim jacket from the back of his swivel chair and heads for the door.

"Hey, Lou," Ray calls out, finishing up his restocking, "where you off to?"

Opening the door, Lou calls back, "Early lunch."

●

It's a short walk to the Garden City station. The streets are quiet, shopkeepers wearing aprons sweep broad side-walks with small brooms. The luncheonettes and diners are mostly empty, the breakfast rush long gone. Pizza places won't open for lunch until eleven. Lou buttons up his jacket and stuffs his hands into his jeans as he walks. It's finally cooling off after a long and hot summer. Fall will be here soon.

He skips up the station steps, pays his $1.60 for a one-way ticket to Penn Station, and waits on the outdoor platform for the train. Commuters made this trip hours ago, so the platform is quiet, just like the streets. Besides Lou there are a few students who look like they just woke up, a senior citizen pushing a silver cart, and a woman rocking a pram back and forth. Lou sits on a bench and closes his eyes until the train arrives.

Ten minutes later, the blue-and-yellow engine pulls into the station. Lou picks an empty car, even though he knows it won't stay empty. There are almost a dozen stops before Manhattan and, by the time the train passes through Kew Gardens and Forest Hills, it will be mostly filled. Sitting by a window, Lou watches Long Island pass by. It's nothing but car dealerships and department stores. Gas stations and muffler shops. Flat mediocrity everywhere he looks. He closes his eyes again.

After a half hour of picking up passengers throughout Queens, the train goes underground. All the passengers get off at Penn Station. Lou walks with the crowd through the low-ceilinged passageway until coming out to a concourse lined with newsstands, food stalls, and information booths. Guys who work on Wall Street are getting shoeshines while old men shuffle through the terminal in trench coats and hats.

The whole building feels squat and claustrophobic. The old Penn Station had been bulldozed so that Madison Square Garden could sit on the station like a hen on an egg. Lou had been through the old Penn Station once when it was in its prime, his family taking the train into the city to see *The King and I* at Radio City. Back then, pulling into Penn Station had been magical, like entering a palace or a castle. Now it feels like going to the dentist.

Turning a few corners, he makes his way to the subway. He approaches a ticket booth, lays down some change, asks for two tokens. The man in the booth looks sleepily at Lou's offer of nickels and dimes.

"I'm sorry, sir. The fare's been increased as of January. Tokens now cost thirty cents."

Cursing Rockefeller, Lou takes back his change and replaces it with a dollar.

"I remember when it cost half that," he says.

"I remember that too, sir." The man gives Lou his tokens and change. "Have a nice day."

To get to the entrance for the 1 train, Lou has to walk through a long tunnel that smells strongly of urine. He places a token in the slot and pushes through the turnstile. The turnstile makes the sound of a noisemaker as he passes. He descends the steps to the downtown train.

The subway platform is hot and muggy; it smells like damp garbage. On the tracks, rats race around various obstacles. Apple cores, broken bottles, candy bar wrappers. Posters on the tiled walls are either peeling or covered with graffiti. Wooden benches are occupied with men sleeping under newspapers, so commuters stand and rest their shoulders against the steel columns.

The train finally arrives, and Lou gets on. Looking around, he sees a few tough-looking teenagers, along with more graffiti. TAKI 183 spans half the car. Lou heard somewhere that the number portion of the tag indicates what street the artist lives on. There are also ads for beer and cigarettes, only you can't read the brand names due to all the scratches, ink, and spray paint. Lou knows the subway can be dangerous. People are mugged or worse. He doesn't care. At the moment, he doesn't have anything worth stealing.

He gets off after two stops. Coming aboveground, he realizes he hasn't been back to New York since that last night at Max's.

After walking down just half a block of Fourteenth Street, he sees more life and color than he has in the month he'd been back in Freeport. Every store has people in it, every corner holds some sort of crowd. He overhears snatches of conversation in different languages. There's laughter coming from one direction and crying from another. Taxis honk and change lanes, messengers zoom by on bikes, delivery boys jog down the street wearing paper hats and carrying coffee and sandwiches. Lou feels his blood pump a little faster. He's home.

Passing a church on the corner of Sixth Avenue, Lou overhears a young Puerto Rican wearing a red windbreaker say to a friend, "I know I'm a sinner, man, but look at this place!" Lou gives a smile as the boy's words ring in his head. Half a block later, Lou hums to himself, "Heavenly Father, I know I have sinned, but look where I've been."

He rounds the corner at Union Square West and heads north. He stops as he approaches Sixteenth Street to look at the building. The Factory's on the sixth floor. It's a narrow structure of ten floors placed between a shorter building to the right and a bigger one on the left. It's so narrow that, when Warhol was shot in '68, the paramedics couldn't fit the stretcher in the elevator. They ended up carrying him down the six flights. When they finally got to the bottom, Andy had lost so much blood, he was paler than anyone had ever seen him (and for Warhol, that was saying something).

Lou walks into the lobby and enters the elevator.

He misses the original Factory, the one on Forty-Seventh. It was so far east there was just one more block before you hit water. It was always cool over there, with either a breeze coming off the East River or shade provided by the Chrysler Building. That's where the Velvet Underground spent a lot of time in '66. Practicing, writing songs, just generally hanging out. It was a wild scene, especially for a kid from Long Island. Drag queens, drugs, cameras filming every moment and Andy, always in the background, making things. Paintings. Films. Trouble. Everyone was either creative or crazy and, after you've been up for three days on speed, you really couldn't tell the difference between the two.

After he fired Warhol as the band's manager, and the Factory moved down to Union Square in '68, Lou didn't come around much. He'd figured out that Andy's promise of fifteen minutes of fame could turn into a death sentence.

The elevator doors open, revealing a sign on the Factory door. KNOCK LOUDLY AND ANNOUNCE YOURSELF. Lou half-heartedly pounds with the heel of his hand and says, "Open up, it's Valerie Solanas."

A minute later, the door slowly opens.

"Lou."

"Andy."

Warhol steps aside to let him enter. Andy's wearing

brown corduroy jeans and a blue work shirt under a fancy plaid blazer. His wig is beige and looks like straw. In the sixties Warhol always wore black leather, along with sunglasses and a shiny silver wig that matched the tinfoil walls of the Factory. Today he has clear spectacles that disappear against his pale and splotchy face. He used to look dangerous. Now he just seems like a rich middle-aged man in New York.

"It's so good to see you," Andy finally says.

He speaks so evenly and without emotion that Lou can't read anything into the words. Was Warhol actually glad to see him, or was he still mad? Lou had stayed away after Andy was shot simply because he didn't know what to do. What do you say to someone who almost died? It was awkward. Warhol took that reticence as a rebuke. He thought that Lou no longer cared.

"You too, Andy."

In the background Lou can hear Maria Callas singing an aria that sounds slightly familiar. Italian, a song sung to a father. Callas had always been the Factory soundtrack, even at the height of the sixties rock scene. There used to also be dozens of conversations happening simultaneously, along with the whirring of a film camera and the sound of Gerard hammering together Brillo boxes. Now, other than opera, all Lou can hear is the rustling of papers coming from a small office just off the Factory entrance.

"How are you *doing*, Lou? I heard you're back on Long Island."

"I'm living at home and working for my dad. It's all very glamorous."

Warhol smiles at his favorite word.

"Written any songs lately?"

"No, Andy. I'm kind of taking a break from all that."

This makes him frown, a fake pout.

"Oh, Lou, you're so *lazy*. You won't be young forever."

Lou knew to expect Andy's disappointment, but that doesn't make it any easier to take. All these years later, Reed still respects Warhol and craves his approval.

"How about you? You still painting?"

Andy grins. "I paint my nails. I paint my eyes every day."

"Andy, quit joking. I hear you're doing great."

Warhol's grin turns into a big smile and his nose seems to burn pink.

"Did you see the retrospective in Pasadena? We went out there. It was *fabulous*. A soup can sold the next day for sixty thousand. Can you believe it?"

As they walk further into the studio, with its bright white walls and floor, Lou sees a few canvases in various states. They're all portraits, people he doesn't know. The paintings are about three by three feet and the images are all square and close-up, the faces looking like a newscaster on TV or a criminal's mug shot.

A man comes out of the small office and approaches them from behind. He says, "The soup can was the highest price ever for a living American artist."

Lou turns around. The man is shorter than Warhol but taller than Lou. He's wearing a suit and glasses. This is Fred Hughes, Warhol's new business manager.

Billy Name had run the old Factory. He was brilliant and crazy in equal measure, an artist as good as anyone else who came to the studio. He's the one who created the silver Factory. He was also the house photographer. At one point, for a year and a half, he refused to leave one of the Factory bathrooms he'd turned into a darkroom. No one could get him to come out. Every morning there would be yogurt and takeout containers outside the bathroom door, but no Billy. Finally, one morning, he was gone. The only thing he left behind was a note pinned to the door.

Dear Andy, I am not here anymore, but I am fine really. With love, Billy

His leaving had left a vacuum. Paul Morrissey stepped in first, and then Fred Hughes. Hughes had gotten his start sweeping the Factory's floors. Now he's in charge.

"Hello, Fred," says Lou.

Hughes just nods in return.

"Everyone thought the price was a prank. That it couldn't be true," Andy continues. "But it was real. And then, did you hear? John Giorno sold a suicide painting for thirty thousand. Cash. But that was directly to a collector, the rat. And to think of all I did for him."

Lou's about to say something when Fred steps between them.

"Andy, don't forget. We're having Yoyo for lunch to talk about a portrait."

"Oh, right." Andy places the first two fingers of his right hand to his chin. "Are we ordering food from Brownies?"

Lou remembers. The health food place on the corner.

Fred chuckles. "I don't think so, Andy. I'm going to order some pasta salads from Balducci's. Now, do you remember the prices? For the portraits, I mean."

Andy looks like he does but doesn't want to say in front of Lou.

"Twenty-five thousand for the first portrait, fifteen for the second," Fred answers. "Ten for the third and five thousand for the fourth."

"Volume discount," Lou says. "Andy, that's so generous of you. And to think that everyone says you're cheap."

Warhol smiles.

"Someone's got to bring home the bacon."

Fred shoots Lou a look before retreating back to his office.

When they're alone, Lou says, "It looks like things are going well for you, Andy."

"They are, Lou. They *really* are."

Warhol begins to walk around to the various portraits in the room, moving them from one side to another. In the background the record stops but, a few seconds later, Fred flips it over.

"There will be another exhibition in Paris before the end of the year. And we're going there in a few days to make a new movie."

"Why Paris?"

Andy shrugs slightly.

"We ran out of apartments in New York."

Standing up, Warhol looks out the window. He stares at something in Union Square. Lou just stands there, watching Andy think. Warhol finally turns back to his old friend.

"So, Lou, what brings you all the way out here?"

Reed grins before answering. It seems like such a crazy situation. He's read so many Raymond Chandler novels, but he never expected to be in one himself.

"Do you know anything about a guy named Samuel Donato?"

Warhol stiffens for a second before moving the portraits back to where they had been.

"Oh, Lou. Don't ask about *him*."

"You know—knew him?"

"We all did." Andy stops what he was doing and looks at Lou. "Don't you remember?"

"Me?" Lou steps back. "I never met the guy."

"Oh, *sure* you have."

Warhol returns to moving the portraits. When he's done, he walks deeper into the studio. Here the floors and walls are black. Lou follows him.

"Andy, what are you talking about?"

Warhol's facing a wall completely covered in Polaroids. There must be hundreds of them. Maybe a thousand. Andy or Billy Name took a picture of everyone who visited the Factory. It was easier than having them all sit for a screen test. The photos got taped to the wall as a sort of visual guest book. Even from a distance, Lou can make out some of the faces. Bob Dylan. Salvador Dalí. John and Yoko. Mick Jagger. The ones who aren't famous look dirty and hungry.

Warhol finds the photo he's looking for, grabs it from the wall, and hands it to Lou. This one is different because it features two faces.

"That's Donato," Warhol says. "And that is you."

In the picture, Lou has bangs and his hair is straight. In the sixties, he'd found a cream that straightened his curls. He's dressed in his standard uniform from back then: black shirt, black jacket, sunglasses. He's smiling. The other figure, also smiling, towers over Lou. He must be six two or six three. He's wearing a suit with wide lapels and a paisley tie with a knot as big as an apple. The man's eyes have a sort of glassy look and his hair, while short, segues into long sideburns that frame a square jaw. It's the same person from the *Times* article Lou saw in his father's office that morning. Donato, the dead man.

"Poor Lou," Andy sighs. "You and that memory of yours."

Lou looks from the Polaroid to Andy.

"When was this taken?"

Warhol shrugs again.

Lou examines the photo more closely. He can see a painted silver pay phone in the background. This means it was taken at the old Factory. It must have been some time in '66.

"What else do you remember about him?"

"Sammy?" Andy sounds bored and turns back to the photos. He looks them over as if they were a stamp collection. "He wasn't a nice man."

"Then why did you give him a painting?"

Warhol turns around, his face holding a look that Lou can't quite place. And then, as if life were just TV and he can change the channel in his head to a new show, Andy softens and becomes friendly again.

"Oh, just, you know—for fun."

"Andy, you wouldn't even pay people who appeared in your films. Why would you give a complete stranger one of your paintings? They were really valuable, even back then."

One of Andy's hands nervously runs a finger up and down the lines of his corduroy pants.

"Oh, Lou, there was *so* much going on in those days.

So many paintings. So many people. I can't keep track of them all."

"But you said you remembered him." Lou raises the Polaroid. "Why?"

Warhol's about to answer when Fred Hughes returns.

"Andy, we need to get ready."

Warhol walks slowly back toward the main part of the studio. Fred and Lou follow. Passing a large table filled with photos and small tubs of paint, Andy notices a big box.

"Oh, that just came in from Chromacomp," Fred says. "The boy just dropped it off."

Andy opens the box like a kid opening a birthday present. He pulls out a large positive proof of a photo. It's an older man Lou doesn't recognize.

"Halston," Andy says. "Isn't he *divine*?"

Lou raises his eyebrows as Warhol examines the sheet.

"Good, no middle tones," Warhol says. "The last one had too many middle tones. I just need the very light and the very dark tones."

Lou steps forward and says, "Andy?"

Fred also steps forward. Instead of speaking, he just raises his arm and taps his watch. It's a very nice watch.

"I'm so sorry, Lou," Warhol says, "but we have *people* coming over. Thanks for stopping by."

As Fred and Andy walk him to the front door, Lou realizes he's still holding the Polaroid. His thumb covers part of Donato's face.

"Don't worry, Lou," Andy says, grinning. "You can keep that. A present from me."

In the hallway, Fred presses the button for the elevator

before retreating back into the Factory. He shoots Lou another look as he closes the large door.

•

Stepping onto the sidewalk, Lou regrets the jacket. The sun is now high in the sky and he can feel himself begin to sweat. He glances at his watch. 1:21. Lou had told Ray that he was heading for an early lunch, but in fact he hasn't eaten anything since breakfast. He decides to head to Max's for a bite.

Lou jaywalks and cuts across the top of Union Square Park. From the corner of Seventeenth and Park Avenue South, he can see the sign. White lowercase words against shiny black plastic, *max's kansas city*. Below this, smaller, *steak lobster chick peas*.

He stands for a second under the long black awning, enjoying the cool of the shade. At night there's always a doorman corralling the rowdy crowd, but at lunch Chemical Bank next door gets more foot traffic than Max's. Lou walks in.

The restaurant is long and thin, like a railroad apartment. Stairs just inside the entrance lead to the second floor and booths line the wall on the right for half the space. The bar is to the left. The kitchen is located in the middle of the room, with more booths and tables opposite. Another staircase toward the back also leads to the second floor. Outside the kitchen is a phone booth and a jukebox. Just beyond that is the back room.

Lou had spent countless hours in the back room as part of Andy's entourage. Shortly after the restaurant opened in '65, Warhol commandeered the space for him and his superstars. Candy Darling. Edie Sedgwick. Holly Woodlawn. Joe Dallesandro. They were all there, night after night. The back room's only about thirty by thirty feet, with tables that have red napkins and red table-cloths, but everybody crowded in. Andy always sat at the round table with the black vinyl banquette.

Today there are just a dozen people in the whole place. A few couples sit in booths and a handful of others are at the bar. Things don't start jumping at Max's until seven or eight. Until then, it's just starving artists filling up on the free happy-hour buffet while insurance salesmen and admen drink and wait for their trains back to the suburbs.

As he slides into a booth behind the table in the front window, Lou waves at a waitress he recognizes. She waves back before disappearing into the kitchen. When she reappears a minute later, she's carrying two plates laden with lobsters the color of a fire engine. After dropping off the lobsters, she gives Lou a menu.

"Be right back," she says quickly, responding to a customer who's hailing her like a cab. He watches her, the short black miniskirt floating from side to side as she walks. The waitresses all wear black miniskirts and black tank tops. The skirts are so short that, whenever a girl leans over, her ass is on full display. The waitresses don't seem to mind. It brings them bigger tips.

"Lou!"

He feels a slap on the back. It's Mickey Ruskin, the owner. Mickey is tall and skinny with a dark head of hair. Everybody calls him Ichabod Crane.

"Mickey, how ya doing?"

"Not bad, not bad. Hey, think you might catch that bill in a couple of months?"

Mickey lets all the regulars run up tabs that are rarely called, much less collected. In the sixties, when the restaurant was primarily a hangout for artists, they'd pay their debts with paintings or sculptures. The third floor is filled with canvases. Mickey fed everybody.

"Soon," Lou says, then grins. "Soon."

Mickey grins back, showing a broken silver tooth.

"Wayne," Mickey calls out to the bartender, a big guy wearing a Hawaiian shirt. "Get my friend here a boilermaker."

Lou's about to protest, saying it's too early, but stays quiet.

Mickey gives him a final slap and moves on. The waitress returns carrying a pad of paper and a yellow pencil covered in chew marks. At Max's, even the waitresses take speed.

"How ya doing, Lisa?"

"I'm good, but we miss you, Lou. It was fun having you around."

He'd spent most of the summer at Max's. The Velvet Underground had a two-week residency that started in June but had stretched into late August. And even though he'd always loved hanging out in the back room with Andy and the Factory crowd, he resented being the house band. The stage upstairs is tiny, with just enough space for their instruments and amps. Most nights it was just a disco; they'd only started having live music last year. The staff call the second floor Siberia. It's where they put the bridge-and-tunnel crowd and the tourists. His manager had also put a prohibition on the slow songs Lou wanted to play. He ended up blowing out his voice every night, forcing him to let Doug Yule take lead vocals on a bunch of songs they were recording for their fourth record during the day up at Atlantic.

Moe, their drummer, also had to sit out the gigs because she was pregnant. As a replacement, they'd hired Doug's younger brother. Billy was a kid, just sixteen. Still in high school, he wasn't allowed to sit at the bar but, for some reason, they let him sit behind the drums. He was a rock kid who played everything fast. Even "Pale Blue Eyes" turned into a dance song behind Billy's frantic beat.

"So, what'll you have?"

Lou quickly examines the menu. He's heard the steaks are aged in coolers in the basement. The lobsters probably come from the Hudson. He plays it safe and orders a burger. She writes it down, gives him a wink, and returns to the kitchen.

The bartender comes over and delivers a beer and a shot of whiskey. Lou takes a sip of each and instantly feels better. The jukebox won't be turned on until later, so instead the room is filled with classical music from WNCN. Lou takes another long sip of the beer and the whiskey.

A tall and skinny busboy with curly hair like Lou's approaches and begins to put dirty dishes from a nearby table into a black plastic tub.

"Hiya, Jonathan," Lou calls out.

The busboy looks up. His eyes get wide when he sees who it is.

"Lou! How are you?" He leaves the tub and comes over to Lou's table. "I heard you quit the band. Please tell me it's not true."

Jonathan's from Natick and has the thickest Boston accent Lou's ever heard. That's where they'd met. Jonathan used to show up at the Boston Tea Party whenever the Velvet Underground played there, which was a lot. Jonathan had even opened for the band once, performing with just an acoustic guitar. He's now working at Max's and trying to get together a band of his own.

"Sorry, it's true."

Jonathan slaps at the table. A dish of dried chickpeas upends, scattering pods across the tabletop like marbles.

Mickey comes down from upstairs on his way to the kitchen.

"Hey, Richman," he barks, "get back to work."

The busboy mutters, "See ya, Lou," and goes back to clearing dishes.

Lisa drops off the burger and Lou tears into his lunch. It's been a long morning and all he had at home was coffee and toast. He has three bites left when he feels someone approach.

"Well, look what the cat dragged in."

He looks up to see a chubby woman with freckles and piercing baby blue eyes. She's carrying a tape recorder in one hand and a Polaroid camera in the other. Around her left shoulder is an expensive-looking purse. Her clothes might have come from the Navy Surplus store, but the scarf around her neck is from Saks Fifth Avenue.

"Hello, Duchess."

Her real name is Brigid Berlin, though no one calls her that. She was given the name Duchess because her parents are rich and famous socialites who know everybody. Most of the crowd who hung around Warhol were runaways or addicts, lost kids who only pretended to be famous or important. Brigid is the real thing. The other name people knew her by was Brigid Polk. "Polk" stood for *poke*, which came from the fact that she liked to give injections of amphetamines to herself or anybody else. Sometimes she did this without the knowledge or consent of the person being poked. She would just sidle up to someone at a party and give them a shot through their clothes.

As she's sitting down, she asks, "Mind if I join you?"

Lou nods vaguely.

Brigid settles into the booth, setting the tape recorder on her left and the camera on her right. Notebooks and pens poke out the top of the sagging purse. She's working on her cock book and came to Max's looking for volunteers.

As he's finishing the whiskey, Lou sees Brigid's hand going for the tape recorder. She has one finger on Play and another on Record.

"No, Duchess," Lou says. "Don't tape me. Not today."

She pouts for a second but then perks up.

"Haven't see you since August. What are you doing back here?"

He takes a sip of beer before answering.

"Stopped by the Factory. Wanted to talk to Andy."

She pouts again.

"I never go down there anymore. That was last year."

"I thought you two were close."

"He's been different ever since that Fred showed up. Andy used to be an artist. Now he's just a businessman."

"Come on, he was always like that. Selling paintings. Selling himself."

Lou finishes the last of his burger.

"Selling *us*," Brigid adds, grabbing a few of the french fries that are left. "And now he just wants to make money with those damn portraits. He's always trying to get me to refer my parents' society friends. Do you know he offered to give me a painting? I said forget it. I told him I wanted a washing machine instead."

That makes him remember Donato. Lou pulls the photo from his pocket.

"Hey, Brigid, does this guy look familiar?"

She takes the Polaroid and examines it. While she's looking, Lou spots a couple of bankers enter Max's, take a look around, and quickly exit.

"Doesn't look like anyone *we'd* hang out with."

"Forget that," Lou snaps. "Do you know him?"

"No," she says, handing back the picture, "doesn't ring a bell. Who is he?"

"Was," Lou says, taking the snapshot. "He's dead."

Brigid ignores this and points at the photo.

"Fucking Polaroids. Andy got that from me. Tape-recording things too. Do you know that when I played him tapes of me talking to my mom on the phone, he taped my tapes?" She smiles and waves at a waitress. The waitress blows her kiss. "Said he's going to turn it into a play. Can you believe that?"

Easing out of the booth, he mumbles, "I guess I can believe anything."

He's putting on his jacket when Brigid says, quietly, "You know, I taped that last night. Your concert."

"Here?" Lou points to the ceiling. "That Sunday? Our last show?"

"Yes." She strokes her tape recorder as if it were a pet, running a finger around the *O* in SONY. "Both sets. It's actually a riot. Jim Carroll was there and talked over you a bit, and a few other people came by and said things too. It's fabulous."

Lou looks out onto Park Avenue South. The sidewalk is in shadows, the sun having disappeared behind the sky-scrapers.

"You want to come over? I can play them for you."

Lou feels light-headed in a good way. The beer and whiskey on his tongue make him wish he had a cigarette.

"Come on," she says. "I'll even give you a poke."

Lou lays down five dollars and says, "Let's go."

●

Brigid lives in a small apartment on East Twenty-Second stuffed with books, magazines, pictures, cassette tapes, cameras, and microphones. She's a pack rat, but she also has a system. Everything is labeled. Everything has a place. It's the cleanest cluttered apartment Lou has ever seen.

Dropping her purse onto an end table, she says, "Do you want some grape soda?"

"No, thanks."

"You want a downer?"

Lou just shakes his head and tries to find a place to sit that's not covered in photos or tapes. He moves a stack of paintings and sits down on the edge of a couch.

"You still doing those?" He points to the canvases.

"The tit paintings? They always sell."

Lou laughs.

"I don't know, Brigid. I think an artist should be able to make money with their clothes on."

"I was never nude, just topless." She lifts a chair and a bunch of Polaroids fall to the parquet floor. Lou recognizes half the faces as belonging to the kids who hang around Warhol. "Did you really move back home?"

He leans forward and rests his elbows on his knees.

"My dad wants me to be an accountant. Get married. Move to the suburbs, just like he did."

Brigid smiles.

"And *my* mother wanted me to be a slim, respectable socialite. Instead, I became an overweight troublemaker."

Lou laughs and sits up.

"Listen, where are those tapes?"

Her eyes brighten. Brigid records pretty much every minute of her life. She tapes phone calls and dinner conversations. She takes a Polaroid of everyone she meets. Mug shots, the same as Andy. If it's happening to her, she feels it should be documented. Not that she has any grand plan for what she's going to do with it all.

After a minute of rooting around, she finds the tape in a box labeled MAX'S. There are two tapes, one for each set. The band played at 11:30 p.m. and 1:00 a.m., five nights a week. She presses Play and then leaves the room to prepare the mixture of amphetamine and vitamins.

The first minute is just crowd noise and the band tuning up, Billy hitting various cymbals. Lou can hear himself talking to someone, probably Sterling or Doug. Then he addresses the crowd.

"Good evening, we're called the Velvet Underground. You're allowed to dance, in case you don't know."

He said this because, except for the first couple of

nights when all their friends came—they hadn't played in New York for years—the rest of the shows had been quiet. The small dance floor was usually empty while the few people in attendance sat with their drinks in booths, clapping politely. It was a hip Manhattan crowd, impossible to impress. Lou had never wanted to be a nightclub act, telling jokes and stories in between songs like Elvis in Vegas. As July dragged into August, he'd had enough.

The first song is "I'm Waiting for the Man." Without Moe providing the steady backbeat, it's fast and frantic. There'd actually been a decent crowd that last night, even if it was a Sunday. His parents were there, as was a young student named Bettye he'd just started dating. She's now in Europe and won't be back for another couple of months.

As Brigid reenters the room with a plate holding two syringes, Lou stands up and unbuckles his jeans.

Pulling them down, she asks, "Right side or left?"

"Brigid, not so low."

She just laughs.

"Come on, Lou. You know I put everybody's heads in the right place."

She gives him a quick stab with the needle, injecting the mixture. Lou closes his eyes and feels the rush. It's perfect timing since the next song is "White Light/White Heat." That had always been a fast song, but that night it was blazing. Lou figures they were playing quickly because they couldn't wait to get the hell out of there. At least that's how it had been for him.

Lou sits down as Brigid stands up and shoves down her canvas pants.

"I'm running out of places to inject." She finally finds

a suitable spot and plunges in the needle. As she's pressing down the plunger with her thumb, she says with a grin, "And they wondered why in the hospital I got hepatitis."

The next song is "I'm Set Free." Lou turns off the tape recorder. It's not the song he wants to hear right now.

"Lou, it's the other set, anyway. That's the one that's a riot. Jim's sitting with me and he's talking about *Patton* and trying to score some pills. You *have* to hear it."

Lou knows he should leave—stuff's piling up on his desk back at the office—but he's starting to feel good. When he leans into the couch, he feels the photo of Donato in his pocket.

Brigid swaps out cassettes and fast-forwards a few times. Lou hears snippets of "Sweet Jane," "I'll Be Your Mirror," and "Candy Says." Now that he's left the group, he's not sure if anyone will ever hear those songs again. Five years, wasted. Gone.

Brigid cues up "Femme Fatale." She says, "It's after this, I think."

She leaves the room to prepare another shot. As the song ends, and the last chord fades amid polite applause, Lou hears a voice. It doesn't belong to Brigid, Jim Carroll, or anyone else he knows. A man's voice says, loud and clear into the portable microphone, "Lou, I saw you kill him. Why did you do it?" Then the band goes into "Some Kinda Love."

Brigid comes back into the room. She points to the Sony.

"It's a riot, right?"

He just nods, lost in thought. Lou pictures Donato, dead in his apartment. Then he thinks of the Polaroid of them together. He tries to remember. *Did I have anything to do with his death?*

"Hey, Duchess," Lou says. "What do they give you these days for murder?"

When she sits down, the chair creaks.

"Hell, they only gave Valerie three years for shooting Andy."

"Brigid, I'm serious."

She shrugs and lifts her blouse, looking for another place to give herself a shot. Her belly, filled with stretch marks and pin pricks, looks like a map.

"They'd send you to Sing Sing, I bet."

"And then what?"

As Brigid plunges in another syringe she answers, plainly, "The electric chair."

●

Leaving Brigid's, Lou walks in a daze. Any positive feeling provided by the shot disappeared when he heard that voice on the tape. Who said that? And what did that person know? Lou racks his brain, trying to think back to his days at the Factory. Why couldn't he remember anything about Donato? After walking for a few aimless blocks, he looks up. He's crossing Twenty-Fifth Street.

He remembers the name on the receipts he'd seen in Donato's file. Twenty-Third Street Storage. The address had been in the West 500s. That puts it across town, over near Ninth or Tenth Avenue. Almost to the West Side Highway. Lou hails an old Checker cab, the black-and-white pattern running along the side of the vehicle and above the doors and windshield. A blue sticker on the rear window says PLEASE DO NOT SLAM DOOR. Getting in, Lou makes sure he doesn't.

After cutting through the crosstown traffic, the taxi pulls up to the address. Lou gives the driver a dollar and tells him to keep the change.

The building is made out of orange brick that goes up nine stories. There are two loading docks to the left and a blue door on the right that has a weathered sign that says OFFICE. A bigger sign above has the name of the business enclosed inside a big neon box. Lou walks toward the door, not sure what he's going to say when he gets inside.

Opening the door, he sees an old man sitting behind a desk.

"Yes, how can I help you?"

Lou looks around. The office consists of a few chairs and a counter behind which is the desk and the old man. On the walls are diagrams and dimensions of storage spaces. A handwritten sign reads *Packing material available for a fee*. To the left of the door Lou just entered is a watercooler, and to the right of that is another door that has a square pane of glass at the top. Lou looks through the window and sees a long corridor of doors.

"Yeah, I just . . ."

He stops, not quite sure what to say or ask. He has Donato's photo, but doesn't think that will help him much here.

"Are you looking to open an account?"

Lou approaches the counter. There's a sign-in sheet on a clipboard. A blue ballpoint pen is attached to the clipboard with brown twine. Lou can see on the old man's desk the same receipts he'd found in the file that morning.

"No, actually. I, uh, already have one."

The old man opens a drawer and retrieves a weathered lockbox.

"Name?"

"Reed."

"Can I see some identification?"

As the old man gets up and shuffles toward the counter, bringing the lockbox with him, Lou takes out his driver's license. Covering his first name, he flashes it quickly. The old man nods and opens the lockbox. After a bit of searching, he pulls out an index card along with a key.

"Ah, here you are." He offers the key. "It's one of our largest spaces."

The key has a number written on it in what looks like red fingernail polish: 919.

"Please sign in." The old man points to the clipboard.

Lou picks up the pen. He has to write down the time, date, and number of the storage space. He writes his name as *Mr. Reed*.

The old man nods to the door with the window.

"Elevator's just inside there. If you need the freight elevator, it takes a special key."

Lou pushes the clipboard toward the old man.

"No thanks."

Lou enters the hallway and calls the elevator. While he waits for it to arrive he notices, at the end of the long hallway, a large gaping space the size of his parents' garage. That must be for the freight elevator.

The smaller elevator arrives. The ninth floor looks just

like the first floor except the doors are farther apart; 919 is almost all the way to the end. Just beyond is the entrance to the freight elevator, the opening covered with a chain-link gate. Lou inserts the key and opens the lock. At first the door seems stuck but, after putting his weight into it, the large metal door opens with a deafening creak.

Toward the front, Lou can see a few items. A chair. Some end tables. A couch. Mattresses lean against the wall. The rear is hidden in shadows. He feels for a light switch. A bare light bulb illuminates the overstuffed space. Lou sees bookshelves, lamps, dining room chairs stacked to the ceiling. A long dresser that looks like an antique. Lou turns sideways and inches his way into the space.

There's a desk and another dresser. Lou opens various drawers, but they're all empty. He opens the doors of an armoire, but it's empty too. The whole room is filled with objects that could have belonged to anyone. There are no books or clothes, no papers or photos. There's no trace of Donato himself. It's as if an atom bomb had vaporized everything having to do with the man, leaving only furniture behind.

Toward the back, he sees it. A large canvas. He hasn't seen any other sort of art or picture, so he figures this is the Warhol. But it's facing the back wall, so he can't be sure. Even though it's big, probably four by five feet, Lou manages to lift it above a headboard and carry it toward the hallway.

As he's backing out from the rear of the space, carrying the painting, he knocks something with his shoulder, a rug that was rolled up and standing on its end. It falls into the hallway.

Lou sets the painting down. He instantly recognizes it. An electric chair, black against a silver background. It's from Warhol's *Death and Disaster* series. Andy had done dozens of paintings about car crashes, murders, executions. The one he'd mentioned that John Giorno had sold for thirty grand was from the same series. This one has to be worth as much, if not more.

Turning from the painting, he looks at the carpet that had fallen open. It's a small white shag floor rug about the same size as the painting. In the middle, off center, is a dark stain. The spot is purple, almost black. From nowhere, a fly appears and begins buzzing around the stain. Lou leans in and sniffs. The mottled carpet smells sour, almost rotten. Lou gags.

He stands up and looks again at the painting. It's too big to take with him. Even if he managed to get it in a taxi, he doesn't have enough money to get all the way back to Long Island. Trying to take an original Warhol on the subway doesn't seem like a good idea either—he won't make it out of Manhattan. He places the painting back into the space, leaning it against a box spring.

Lou turns to the carpet. When he rolls it back up, he sees that whatever spilled had bled through to the back. He balances the rug on top of an end table and, not knowing what else to do or what to look for, decides to head back to Freeport.

He attempts to close the door, but the rug is poking out. He pushes the rug in further, but it's hitting a dresser farther back and won't move. Lou tries to kick the end table, hoping that will also move the dresser. It seems to work. Everything moves back about an inch. He kicks two more times. On the third try, something falls from the bottom of the end table. Lou squats down to see what it is.

A false bottom to the end table's drawer has come loose and hit the floor. Two things fell along with it. One is an old address book with a leather cover. The other is a silver film can, about the size of a 45 record. Lou picks up both items. The film can is heavy, something is inside. On the front is a sticker that says at the top AWE. In faded ink below this is a date: 11/19/66.

Lou tucks both items under an arm, gives the rug a final shove, and closes and locks the door.

Downstairs, the old man asks, "Did you find what you were looking for?"

Lou doesn't answer. He just signs out on the clipboard, returns the key, and heads back to Long Island.

WEDNESDAY

L OU SITS DOWN at his desk with Donato's address book. Only Sheldon Mayer, Moira, and Jeanie are in the office. All the other desks are unoccupied, their type-writers shrouded in dustcovers. The whole room is quiet. Sheldon's meeting with Sidney Reed in his office and Moira and Jeanie are both looking over paperwork while keeping one eye on the door. They're hoping someone will come in they can talk to. No one does any real work before ten.

The address book is about four by six inches. It's not the cheap kind you get at the drugstore for forty cents and keep near the phone. It looks expensive. The leather cover also looks worn.

Flipping through the pages, Lou notices there are only first names. Also, most listings have just a phone number, or an address, but rarely does an entry have both. Only one name has an address and a phone number. Someone named Kathy from Fairfield, Connecticut. She also seems to be the only listing that's not in New York City. Another peculiar thing is that her name is scratched out. Thick black lines cut across her information in slashed horizontal pen marks.

Lou also notices that nothing is in alphabetical order. Someone named Jackie is in the *K* section and a Timothy is in the *D*'s. At first Lou suspects that the first names have been placed in the section that correspond to their missing last names, but when he discovers himself in the *H*'s, he knows this isn't the case.

Lou slowly runs his finger over the three letters that make up his first name. The number doesn't mean anything to Lou. CA 6-6150. He had moved a lot in the sixties. He lived for a while with John Cale at his loft on Ludlow. Then he moved to that dump near Pitt Street. After that he lived at Seventh and West Twenty-Eighth, in the Fur District. The whole block smelled of hides, but it was cheap.

"Maybe it's not even me," he says out loud, "maybe it's another Lou."

Audrey, just arriving, looks over eagerly. She thinks that he's making small talk, that he wants to chat. But then her expression changes. Lou never wants to chat with anyone.

He picks up the book and holds it close to his face, examining Donato's writing. The letters are strong and precise, all capitals. And yet, even though the pages have lines, the names and numbers are often written at odd angles. What's also strange is that some pages are blank while others hold half a dozen names. Lou figures this was more of a notebook than an address book, something Donato always had on hand. He scribbled the names of people as he met them, where he met them. It would have fit easily into the breast or hip pocket of a blazer.

Flipping through the book a second time, Lou sees Andy's name. He knows this is Warhol, even if it's written in the *G*'s, because he recognizes the phone number for the Factory on Forty-Seventh Street. This makes him check all the addresses. None of them mean anything, though a few seem slightly familiar. Under *Q* is the name Max and an address, 213 Park Avenue South. That's Max's Kansas City. This tells Lou that Donato had been more than just a tourist passing through the Factory scene. So why doesn't he remember him?

After glancing through the book for a third time, Lou wonders why it had been hidden in the end table. Was Donato the one who had hid it, or had whoever moved all that stuff into storage been the one to stash it in the secret compartment? And, really, why hide it at all? It's not a crime to write down names and phone numbers, or to keep a list of addresses. And what about the film can? Why was that in there as well?

Lou pulls out the Polaroid of him and Donato that Andy had given him the day before. There's something about Donato's eyes that unnerve Lou. They're small and cold, like glass. There's nothing behind them.

"Hey, Lou." Ray has arrived and is looking for something to do. He sidles up to Lou's desk. "I heard you was in a band?"

Lou quickly shoves the photo back into his pocket.

"Now where'd you hear a thing like that?"

Lou doesn't have to ask. He knows the girls gossip about him. Ray had all but admitted this yesterday with his crack about Creedmoor.

"Yeah, Ray, I was in a band."

"You, like, have records out? Play concerts?"

Lou considers this.

He thinks back to the weeks spent at the Matrix and

Max's Kansas City. Had those been concerts? How about the happenings Warhol staged, where Gerard Malanga whipped Mary Woronov while Nico crooned and Andy showed films on the band? Those definitely weren't concerts. And then there was that first gig at the high school in New Jersey where they played "Heroin" to stunned students. Lou gives the only answer he can.

"Yes, we released records."

This satisfies Ray for about a second.

"What did you sound like?"

"Rock and roll, Ray."

"Like Alice Cooper? Deep Purple?"

"Knock it off with that plastic shit, man. That might as well be the Monkees." Pushing aside the address book, he asks, "You ever hear of the Jesters?"

"No." Ray grins and scratches at his polyester shirt.

"The Diablos? Johnny Ace? The Spaniels?"

He just shakes his head again, no.

"Get back to work, Ray."

He slouches off just as Vera approaches and delivers the morning stack of mail. She places it next to the even bigger stack Lou hadn't gotten to the day before. By now, the office is full. The day has officially begun. Secretaries all sip coffee and talk, while Sheldon Mayer sits looking annoyed because the girls are chatting instead of working. Ray starts talking to Jeanie, who touches her hair while he brags about his car. Lou cranes his head to see if the door to his dad's office is open. It is.

He grabs the address book and stands up. He wants to confront his father with the address book, demand to see Donato's file again, and try to get to the bottom of whatever all of this is. He pulls the Polaroid again out of his pocket, ready to compare it to the picture from the *Times*. He wants to see if Donato looks more human in that one. Holding the snapshot, he's filled with questions. When had he met Donato? Why was his own name in the dead man's address book? Lou sits back down. He decides he has to solve this mystery on his own. He's never gone to his dad with a problem before, and he doesn't want to start now.

He pulls the phone toward him and opens Donato's book. He tries the first number he comes to, a listing for Jane in the *A*'s. It rings and rings. Lou hangs up. The next two numbers are disconnected. At a listing for Marguerita, the man who answers speaks only Spanish. At the three numbers Lou tries after that, no one's home.

The next name in the book is Sarah. Lou dials. After four rings, someone picks up.

The voice, sleepy. A woman. "Hell-hello?"

"Yeah, uh, hi. I know this is going to seem weird, but my name is—"

"Oh my God."

"Excuse me?"

She says, slowly, *"Lou."*

He loses track of what he was going to say next. He had something planned about Donato and the book, but he goes blank. In the void, she speaks again.

"We should talk."

"Okay," he says. "Where are you?"

As she recites an address, he writes it down on the letter about Donato he hadn't finished typing the day before.

"Fine," he begins, "I'll be there in—"

But she's already hung up.

Lou glances at the address. It looks like he'll be going into Manhattan again.

•

After transferring at West Fourth, Lou takes the D train to the Lower East Side. He comes aboveground at Chrystie and Grand. From the tip of Roosevelt Park, looking south, he can see the new buildings that are going up on the waterfront. There will be two towers, taller than anything else on the island. Crews had started digging out the area in '66 and began on the buildings themselves two years later. A trio of cranes sit on top of each structure, looking like giant spiders. The buildings seem odd, each a perfect square. The south tower is totally enshrouded with scaffolding. The north one appears to be almost done, it has to be sixty or seventy stories already. Lou can't imagine they'll build many more. Floors about midway up are covered in a protective fabric that shines like gold in the late summer light of New York.

Lou starts walking, the address book under his arm. Sarah lives on Orchard between Grand and Canal. He knows the area well. The loft he shared with John Cale is just one block over, on Ludlow. He overshoots Orchard so he can see where he used to live with his bandmate.

Cale had been living there for a while with Tony Conrad. Conrad was a fellow musician, part of Cale's group of avant-garde minimalists and experimenters. The La Monte Young crowd. Conrad left around the time Lou moved in. Some early demos were recorded on an old tape deck Conrad left behind. He also found in the street the book that would give the group their name. It was a cheap paperback about S&M. Lou took one look at the cover and named the band the Velvet Underground.

He heads south at the corner of Ludlow and Grand. It's just down on the left, the first apartment building on the block. Lou looks up to where he'd lived on the fifth floor with Cale. In '64, the whole block was bleak and depressing, the streets always empty. It felt like a no-man's-land. A small shop selling tea on the ground floor supplied the only light for the entire block, a pale-yellow glow. Lou never went inside the shop, never had money for tea.

The rent was twenty-five dollars a month, but that's because it had no heat and the neighborhood was a war zone. Looking around, Lou decides it isn't much better today. The building has been given a fresh coat of paint, but that's already peeling. A few cars are on cinder blocks, missing their tires and, in one case, doors. The handful of shops brave enough to exist have bars on their windows.

In the summer of '65, when the first version of the group got together, it consisted of Cale, Lou, Sterling Morrison, and Angus MacLise. They worked on half a dozen songs, some of which would go on to be part of their setlists for the rest of the decade. Lou had written "Heroin" in college as a poem and had only recently put it to music. It was what first made Cale want to work with him. Not that it was an easy fit. The eventual meshing of Lou's and John's sounds became the template for the first phase of the band. But back then, they were still searching. When Cale sang "Venus in Furs," it resembled an old English folk song, something like "Scarborough

Fair." "I'm Waiting for the Man" had none of its eventual swagger, coming off in these early versions as a country tune with slide guitar. Lou had even written a protest song in the mold of Dylan, complete with harmonica. Lou had always favored rock and roll over folk, but it was New York in the midsixties. Dylan's shadow was hard to escape. He'd seen him, while in college at Syracuse in '63. Lou even sang it like Dylan. In the end, "Prominent Men" never appeared on a record.

At the time he lived here, Lou was still working at Pickwick Records. That's where he'd met both Cale and Conrad. They'd been recruited to be part of a hustle, pretending to be a band playing a song that pretended to be a hit, "The Ostrich." Lou's day job was churning out bad songs for cheap records to be sold in the bargain bins of department stores. It was the only other nine-to-five job he's ever had. That and what he's doing now for his dad. He thinks about both and tries to decide which is worse. At Pickwick, at least he got to play guitar.

He walks down Ludlow and takes a right on Hester. It's a short block, and Lou can see all the way through to the traffic heading north on Allen. Windows are boarded up and no one's around. Less than a hundred years ago, the Lower East Side had been packed with immigrants. Sidewalks swarmed with peddlers selling all manner of things: food, services, themselves. Pushcarts and over-flowing trash cans were everywhere you looked. Now it's a ghost town. Where did all those people go?

Orchard is the same but different. Huge buildings that have seen better days, rusting fire escapes, trees dying from lack of sunlight and the fact that dogs and people keep pissing on them. Only the graffiti is different. Sarah's building is halfway down the block. Walking up the front steps, Lou thinks he smells the remains of a fire. The buzzer is broken, but the door is ajar. He walks up the four flights and knocks.

The door's opened by a woman with strawberry-blond hair and green eyes that are only half-open. She looks like she just woke up, even though it's almost noon. A huge oatmeal-colored cardigan hangs off her slim shoulders, and her legs are like sticks poking out of a pair of cutoff jean shorts covered in multicolored patches.

"Sarah?"

She looks him up and down. When she registers who he is, she opens the door and invites him inside.

The apartment is large, but nearly empty. The furniture consists of an old couch, a filthy upholstered chair, and an end table with a lamp that provides the only light in the room. Paper blinds are drawn over the windows and, even though it's a sunny day, the room is enveloped in shadows. In one corner is a kitchen that has, next to the fridge, a bathtub. The sink's full of dirty dishes and an open cupboard reveals nothing but empty space. There's a pair of men's boots on the floor, and a flannel work shirt hangs from a coat rack.

She finally says, "It's been a long time."

"Has it?"

She laughs. "You don't remember?"

He shakes his head as she sits down on the couch. When he sits in the chair, clutching the address book, the springs squeak. Sniffing at the air, he recognizes the vinegary odor. She even looks like a junkie.

"I'd heard about your bad memory, but I thought you'd remember *me*."

"Why?"

She digs into the pocket of the sweater and pulls out a packet of Benson & Hedges. The white box with the baby blue stripe practically glows in the dim room.

"No reason," she says, lighting a cigarette.

Lou pulls out the Polaroid of him and Donato and hands it to Sarah.

"Know this guy?"

She stares at the photo with contempt, handing it back as soon as she sees who it is.

"Yeah, I knew him."

She takes a long drag on the cigarette. Lou wants one but doesn't want to ask. People who cover their windows with paper don't have cigarettes to spare.

"Knew him from where?"

"From around."

"Around where?"

She exhales and says, wearily, "The scene."

Lou sits up in frustration. This is like talking to a door.

"Who was he?"

She places the half-smoked cigarette in an ashtray and lights another.

"I never knew his real name. Someone heard he'd been in the war, so they started calling him 'the Sailor.' It stuck. Everyone called him that, although I don't know why. All you see on TV is the jungle." She laughs before continuing. "At first he was just around like everybody was back then. There were the Factory kids and the folk scene, underground film people, *New Yorker* people. That's how the Sailor met a bunch of us."

Lou thinks of the suit Donato's wearing in the Polaroid, and all the expensive furniture in storage.

"Was he some rich guy who was just slumming it for kicks?"

He knew the type. Park Avenue trust fund kids who think they're edgy by going up to Harlem to score drugs. Tourists.

"At first, I guess."

"What changed?"

"He showed us who he was."

"Which was what?"

"A monster."

She takes another long drag on the cigarette. Outside there's a siren. The sound echoes between the buildings until it finally disappears somewhere uptown.

"What do you mean?"

"He liked to hurt people, Lou."

"Hurt people, how?"

"With his hands. He was a nasty motherfucker. Got enjoyment out of it. It was, like, a hobby."

Lou shifts in the uncomfortable chair. It squeaks again.

"I don't understand."

The cigarette in the ashtray finally goes out.

"At parties, or at someone's home. People paid to watch. People paid to have it done to them."

"How did you fit in?"

She laughs again, darkly.

"Me? I was one of his props."

She gets up and goes to the kitchen. After opening and closing a few drawers, she comes back and hands him a picture. A color photo of a face, a girl who had been badly beaten. The woman's forehead was cut, dried blood smeared across her scalp. Her eyes were swollen shut, and her cheeks looked like bruised plums. Her lips were split and puffed up.

"Is this you?"

She tries to make a noise like laughter, but it comes out as just a cough.

"You really don't remember?"

Lou tries to think back, but it's just a haze.

"Why?" he says. "Why did you let him do this to you?"

"Why do you think? I needed the money."

Even though Lou places the photo facedown on the arm of the chair, he keeps looking at it.

She lights another cigarette. Exhaling, she says, "You wrote a song about it."

He looks up.

"Which—what song?"

"'She's over by the corner, got her hands by her sides.' That doesn't ring a bell? 'He hit her so hard they thought she might die'?"

He'd written it, but he didn't know where it'd come from. They were just lines that had appeared in his notebook.

"But your name's Sarah."

She takes another drag.

"The Sailor was from down south. Kentucky or something like that. Had a thick accent. When I first met him, and told him my name, he said I looked more like a 'Sally Mae.' So that's what he called me. And that"—she exhales—"is what you put in your song."

"I was there? When he beat you?"

She nods.

"Don't blame yourself. A lot of people were there. I was just . . . the night's entertainment."

While she lights yet another cigarette, Lou remembers the address book. He wonders about the names inside, how they were connected to Donato, and why one of them was crossed out. He begins to flip through the pages.

"What's that?" she says.

Lou answers, as if startled out of a trance, "Names. Phone numbers. I think it belonged to him."

She places the cigarette in the ashtray and reaches for the leather book. She opens it slowly and examines the pages.

"Lou, these names—these people—they're all characters in your songs." She flips through the book, stopping at various pages. "Sally, Jim. Stephanie." She turns a few more pages. "Lisa, Tom."

As Lou sits back in the chair, the photo on the arm falls to the floor. It flips over, and the beaten face stares back at him.

Sarah turns another page, reads the name, and begins to sob.

"Mary, my god, she was just a teenager."

There are footsteps in the hallway. Lou looks to the door but whoever's outside keeps walking.

"Do you know he's dead?"

She wipes away tears and gives the book back.

"Yeah."

"Do you know who killed him?"

She lets out a huge sigh.

"Does it matter?"

"It matters to me."

She gets up and walks to the window, lifting a corner of the stained paper to peer outside.

"I don't know why you're asking me, Lou. You should know more than anybody."

Footsteps again in the hallway. This time, the door opens and two guys enter. They have beards and are wearing sunglasses. They don't seem pleased to see Lou.

Sarah turns and says in a dead voice, "Lou, the fellas. Fellas, this is Lou."

They grunt. Lou grabs the address book and stands up.

"Sarah, I need to know—"

"Lou, I'm tired. And that's all ancient history. He's gone, and that's all that matters."

He's about to protest when each of the guys takes a step forward. Lou puts the address book under his arm and heads for the door.

•

"Lou, nice of you to come back."

He looks up from the typewriter. Ray's grinning at him. Lou didn't return to the office until nearly two. Big stacks of mail were waiting for him, along with nearly a dozen letters that need to be typed. Normally he has to retrieve the handwritten responses from the tray outside his father's office, but someone had seen fit to deliver them right to Lou's desk. That meant someone had been looking for him.

"Don't make fun," Lou says. He pulls the letter he'd been typing out of the typewriter and starts on the next.

By the time Sidney Reed appears at six o'clock to fetch

his son, most of the employees have left. Only Sheldon, Audrey, and Ray are still there, finishing up the last of the day's tasks. As they're leaving, his dad returns briefly to his office to retrieve something. While Lou's waiting, Audrey calls out to him.

"Hey, Lou, I ain't your secretary." She's putting the dustcover on her typewriter. "I'm not paid to take your phone calls."

He walks over as she searches in her piles of paper for the message. She finds the slip and hands it to Lou. Danny Fields called. Lou can come by at noon on Friday to talk.

"Your sister called too."

"Bunny?"

"Yeah, said she was sorry she missed you. She'll see you on Saturday at the club."

Just as Audrey stops speaking, Ray drops the last of his filing to the floor. Papers fly out in all directions.

"Goddamnit, Ray," Audrey calls out, "be more careful!"

Audrey grabs her keys and coat while Ray gets down on his hands and knees to clean up the mess.

"Sister," Lou mumbles to himself. "Ray."

His dad comes out of his office.

"Ready, Son?"

Lou just nods and follows his father to the door, saying the names quietly under his breath. *Sister. Ray.*

They drive home in silence. Turning onto their street, his father finally speaks.

"I spoke to your mother and we're going to order Chinese for dinner. From Pan's. Is that okay with you, Lewis?"

"Yeah, sure."

They pull into the driveway and, for once, his dad gets out of the car first. It takes Lou a few moments to realize they've arrived. He gets out of the car slowly.

Inside, his mom and grandma are sitting at the dining room table looking over a takeout menu. His mom has a pad of paper ready to write down what everyone wants.

"Lou, you just want your usual?" his mom calls out. "Chicken and broccoli?"

"Yeah, yeah," he says under his breath, "whatever."

"I want egg foo young," his grandma says.

While his mom writes down all the dishes, Lou keeps repeating the names in his head, *Sister. Ray. Sister. Ray.*

His dad enters the room, wearing his usual post-work relaxation clothes.

"Hey, Pops," Lou says, but then stops.

"Yes, Lewis?"

Lou steps around his father and goes to his mom.

"Hey, Ma, do you have any of my old records?"

She looks up from the pad of paper. Lou can see his mom's graceful handwriting.

"You mean from high school? I think they're all in your room. I didn't touch—"

"No, I meant *my* records. The, uh, Velvet Underground ones."

Lou had never asked his parents what they thought of his music, and they'd never volunteered an opinion. Whenever he saw his mom and dad over the past couple of years, they always asked how he was doing and casually inquired about the band, but he'd never received any feedback—positive or negative—about the music he'd made since leaving home.

At first, she looks taken aback, but then she smiles shyly.

"Why, yes, Lou. We have them."

She gets up from the table and goes into the living room. His dad loves music and has a big collection of Benny Goodman, big band jazz, and show tunes. His mom opens a cabinet next to the turntable and pulls them out. Three LPs. Two black and one white. Lou reaches for the one in the middle and races back to his room.

He slams the door and rushes toward where his record player sits underneath a window. On the floor is a notebook he uses for lyrics and song ideas, an old tape recorder, and a few paperback books. *City of Night. Naked Lunch. Last Exit to Brooklyn.* He pulls the LP out of the all-black sleeve and places it on the turntable, second side up. He sets the needle on the second song.

The fuzzy three-chord riff fills the room. Outside, Seymour growls. When the lyrics kick in, Lou has to concentrate to hear them. They'd only done one take of the song, and the fact that they'd turned all the instruments up to the maximum meant it was basically just noise. Every sound leaked into and fought with the other.

When the lyrics begin, he tries to find meaning, but it all seems like nonsense. Duck and Sally, pigpens, main lines. *Cooking for the down five.* They're just words, images, crazy shit he'd scribbled in practice. Sometimes, when they played the song live and it would stretch to more than half an hour, Lou would pretend to be a preacher breathing fire. It was all made up, wasn't it?

The song mentions a sailor from Alabama.

"Donato," Lou says to the empty room.

Someone has a gun, takes aim at the sailor, and shoots him. Everybody just seems to stand around and watch, the narrator dryly noting, instead of trying to help, "Don't you know you'll stain the carpet?" Lou thinks about the day before, the storage facility. The shag rug he'd found among Donato's things. The one with the big purple stain.

There's a knock at the door.

"Lou, we're ordering," his mom calls out. "If you want any appetizers, now's the time to tell me!"

He picks up the needle from the record. The room is quiet again.

"No, Mom, I'm good."

He hears her footsteps as she returns to the kitchen.

Lou remembers the date Donato died from the *Times* article. February 10, 1967. He tries to recall where he was then, hoping he'll discover he was out of town when Donato was murdered and thus would have an alibi. The band toured a bit in early '67.

"Boston," he says slowly. "I'm pretty sure we were in Boston."

Lou hears his dad's muffled voice from the other room as he calls Pan's to put in their order.

"It couldn't have been me," Lou reassures himself. "We were on tour. I couldn't have killed him."

He looks at his hands. They're shaking.

THURSDAY

W HEN HIS DAD comes to collect him in the morning, after he doesn't show up for breakfast, Lou shouts through the door that his stomach hurts. He can't go to the office today. Sidney Reed responds with a long sigh. After the Mercedes pulls out of the garage, Lou goes back to bed.

He wakes up a bit after ten. Sitting in bed and running a hand through his mop of curly brown hair, he looks to where an acoustic guitar leans against the closet. The door is ajar and Lou can see a bunch of his old clothes from high school and college. Thin ties and a blue blazer, white buck shoes and faded dungarees. Later, like Warhol, all he wore was black leather. But after John Cale left, the band tried to go pop. This meant smiles, paisley shirts, making an effort. It didn't work. They still didn't get played on the radio and their records didn't sell. By the time they'd played Max's this past summer, the band were dressed in jeans and tennis shoes, just like the audience.

As he reaches for the guitar, Lou notices something else inside the closet. He gets up and grabs two items leaning against a shoebox. The first is blue and leather, about the size of a large paperback book. It's his diploma from Syracuse. On the cover is embossed the school's crest and motto in gold, *Suos Cultores Scientia Coronat.* He forgets what that means—something about knowledge. Lifting the cover, he finds first a certificate announcing he'd made the dean's list for the spring semester of '63/'64. IN RECOGNITION OF SUPERIOR SCHOLARSHIP. This makes him laugh. The only thing he'd concentrated on at college were his discussions with Delmore Schwartz at the Orange Bar.

He puts aside the certificate and looks at the diploma. The whole thing is in Latin, even the date and the name of the school—*Universitas Syracusana.* The only words on the whole thing he recognizes are the two that constitute his name. Lou laughs again. His parents had paid all that money, and he can't even read his diploma.

The other thing he'd pulled from the closet was the yearbook from his final year at Freeport High. The red cover features a huge portrait of Satan—they were known as the Red Devils—along with the word VOYAGEUR and the date of his graduating class in the corner, '59. Flipping through the pages, he sees black-and-white photos of guys with crew cuts smiling for the camera. Cheerleaders sitting on the back of a convertible. Ads for local businesses that have since gone out of business.

Toward the middle he comes across a two-page spread devoted to the seniors' variety show. Lou had played as part of one of his bands, the C.H.D. The name stood for *Dry Hump Club*, backward. Lou had chosen it. In the photo, he's the only one of the four with an instrument. He's wearing, along with the guitar, dark slacks, loafers, a white collared shirt, and a cardigan with wide stripes. They'd performed alongside the Winter Wonderland Chorus Line, which consisted of twenty-two girls doing a dance routine, and the Macongo Cuties, which was just about the same amount of guys in drag doing the same thing.

As he gets to the section of senior portraits, he scans the various faces and reads the signatures that are splayed across the page at odd angles and in different colored inks.

Lots of luck to a great rock & roller.

To the man with the voice.

You're a great singer even though you're a lousy chemistry student.

Best of luck in the recording business.

Even back then, everyone had known what music meant to him. They also knew about the records he'd already made. His band the Jades had released a doo-wop single, "Leave Her for Me." And even though Lou only contributed background vocals, not confident enough to lead the group, he'd written the song. It even became a local hit, getting played on the radio and earning him a few bucks in royalties. Not bad for a high school kid.

He turns more pages. Richard Sigal had written, *Take it slow in N.Y.U.* Lou had only lasted there for half a semester. Just seventeen, it had proved too much for him. He suffered panic attacks, had to drop out, came home. Seeking a cure, his parents had dragged him out to Creedmoor. After six months he was well enough to try again, but this time he opted for Syracuse.

He tosses the yearbook and diploma deep into the closet, finally grabbing the guitar. He strums a few chords and starts singing an old Velvet Underground song.

It's hard being a man
Living in a garbage pail

It feels good to sing and play. He misses it. Even though he'd told friends he was giving up music to become a writer, he still harbors an ambition to make a record of his own. All four of the Velvet Underground LPs had been rushed or flawed in some way, containing experiments that didn't work or compromises that were forced on the band. He wants a chance to finally get it right.

They'd recorded an album's worth of material last year on MGM's dime. He doesn't know if that stuff will ever see the light of day, or even if he wants it to. There's also a bunch of bootlegs there'd been discussions about releasing, live stuff from '69. Lou doesn't know who would buy any of that stuff. It's not like people went crazy for their official records, so who would buy outtakes and live versions?

He reaches to the floor and finds his notebook. He opens it and plays a new song called "Kill Our Sons."

All your drunken congressmen, they're getting out the
   vote
By shipping out the youngest to war in tax-paid votes

The reference to Vietnam makes him think of Donato. Lou looks across the room and sees the address book sitting atop the silver film can he'd taken from the storage locker. He's still shaken by his meeting with Sarah the day before. The possibility that he knows who killed Donato, not to mention that he may have pulled the trigger—and recorded a song about it—makes him uneasy. Lou has to find out what his involvement, if any, had been in the man's death.

He puts down the guitar and emerges from his room. He finds his mom doing dishes while his grandma is still in her robe watching a game show.

"Lou, there you are," his mom says. "Are you feeling better?"

"Yeah, Ma, it's nothing."

He sits down on the couch. The vinyl slipcover feels cool against his striped pajamas. On TV, Monty Hall is talking to a man in a chicken costume. His grandma mumbles, "Don't go for door number two. Take the cash."

His mom shouts from the kitchen, "Son, can I get you anything?"

"Yeah, some coffee and toast, Ma," he shouts back. "And maybe some eggs. Thanks."

The TV goes to a commercial.

"I like the commercials," his grandma says.

"Me too, Bubbie," Lou says. "They're so short, and they've got to get to you really fast."

Seymour's scratching at the back door, so Lou lets him in. He plays with his dog in the living room until his food is ready.

Sitting down to his late breakfast, he realizes how hungry he is. He didn't have much dinner last night. As his mom reenters the room to drop off a small glass of orange juice, he says, "Hey, Ma, can I borrow the car for a bit this afternoon?"

"Sure, Lou, where do you need to go?"

He finishes off the eggs and reaches for the final triangle of toast.

"Levittown," he says, chewing. "I want to visit an old friend."

•

He'd seen Moe right before he quit the band. She came in from Long Island for one of the shows at Max's. It was the first time she'd left the baby with a sitter. She'd been out of the band ever since she got pregnant. In addition to sitting out the summer shows at Max's, she hadn't played on what was looking to be the final Velvet Underground album.

As she and Lou sat on the stairs outside the club, before the group played their first set, he told her about his intention to leave. She tried to talk him out of it, but he couldn't be deterred. He'd made up his mind and no one was going to get him to change it.

Looking back, he realizes what a mistake it had been to keep going when she needed time off. They should have waited. If they had, everything would have turned out differently.

It's a short drive to Levittown. He takes Meadowbrook State Parkway to Route 24. He'll be there in twenty minutes. Maybe less. Pulling into traffic, he turns on the radio. "Cracklin' Rosie" by Neil Diamond fills the huge car. Lou turns off the radio.

He hates driving the Lincoln. It's black and huge and handles poorly. Besides, it looks like a hearse. He's also not a good driver and he knows it. He doesn't even have a license. It was revoked years earlier after he smashed into a tollbooth. He'd always meant to get it back, but living in Manhattan, you don't need or want a car. Besides, he can't afford one.

Moe lives just a few blocks from where she grew up, which is the house where Lou first met her. Sterling Morrison had recommended her since he'd known Moe's older brother at Syracuse. The group was desperate, their first gig was fast approaching. Lou went all the way out to Long Island to audition her. She played for him in her room, using just a bass drum and a snare. It was all she had. Lou just nodded, said, "Okay, that's good," and—just like that—she was in the group.

Turning onto Moe's street, Lou thinks that the houses here look even more cookie-cutter than in Freeport. He didn't think that was possible. He parks the Lincoln and approaches the small A-frame house. The driveway is empty. Lou figures Moe's husband is at work.

As he nears the door, he hears the baby crying. He considers turning around, but figuring he's come this far, he knocks on the cheap metal screen door.

Moe appears with the baby on her hip. Her face lights up when she sees it's Lou.

"Honeybun!"

She opens the door.

"Moesy," Lou says as he enters.

Somehow, the house seems even smaller on the inside than it looks from the outside. The living room is tiny. In the dining room, Lou spots a high chair, a bassinet, and a table covered with dirty dishes. All the furniture is either cheap or old, and the air holds a faint odor of piss. It reminds him of the Lower East Side.

"Lou, it's so good to see you!"

He sits down on the couch while Moe perches herself on a chair and bounces her baby girl on a knee. Moe looks tired and is still carrying baby weight. Her hair, so short when she was in the band—in the early days, no one could tell if she was a boy or a girl—is now so long it almost touches her shoulders. The baby gazes at Lou skeptically.

Moe is the only member of the group he's kept in contact with. John Cale is off producing bands and making solo LPs, and Sterling Morrison is busy at City College getting a degree in literature. Besides, he's always been closest to Moe. He'd protected her, the same as he'd done for his sister.

"What brings you out here on a weekday? I thought you were working for your dad now."

"Took a day off. Wanted to come say hi."

"Well, how nice."

The baby places her hand in her mouth and gnaws. Lou fights the urge to look away.

"Actually, I had a couple of questions. About the band."

"Sure, shoot."

"What do you remember about 'Sister Ray'? Like, when I came in with the lyrics."

She thinks about this.

"You mean where it came from?"

He nods.

"I don't know, Lou," she laughs, "you tell me."

He thinks back to the lyrics. The character in the song who murders the sailor is named Cecil.

"Did you—did we—know anyone named Cecil?"

She considers this.

"I always thought that was because of that jazz guy you liked."

Lou had a radio show while he was at Syracuse called *Excursion on a Wobbly Rail*, named after a track by Cecil Taylor.

"I guess so. You remember anything else about the song?"

She smiles wide.

"I sure loved to play it."

Lou digs into his pocket and produces the Polaroid of him and Donato. He hands it to Moe.

"Does this guy look familiar?"

She looks at the picture but quickly hands it back.

"No, I don't think so. Who is he?"

"It's not important. Listen, do you remember where we were in February of '67?"

She laughs again.

"What, are you trying to establish an alibi?"

Lou tries to laugh.

"Something like that."

Moe gets up.

"I have some old appointment books. I used to keep track of shows and things like that. Let me check."

She looks at the baby, and then at Lou. Moe decides the baby will be better off in the bassinet. She drops off her daughter and then retreats to somewhere else in the house. She returns a minute later with a couple of small day planners. Lou has seen similar ones around his dad's office.

"February," Moe says, sitting back down, "sixty-seven. Let me see. Ah, here we are."

She hands the book to him. The band played in Medford on the fourth and Williamstown on the seventeenth. Two weekend dates, the first a Saturday and the second a Friday. There's no way they would have been up there that whole time. The group barely had money to travel to Massachusetts in the first place, let alone stay up there for a week between shows. This meant that Lou had been in New York when Donato was killed.

"You find what you were looking for?"

He hands back the book.

"Sort of."

While Lou stares out the window, trying to piece together his memory, Moe flips through the day planner.

"These were crazy times." She points at a row of days in January. "God, the record still hadn't come out yet, remember? Even though we'd finished it the year before."

He nods.

"We never did get paid for that, did we? I used to have to chase Andy around just to get money for gas to get home." She turns more pages, points at more days. "Here's where I had to take a job typing just to make ends meet."

This hits too close to home, since Lou is now doing the same for his father.

"Typing what?"

"That book Andy published. The novel. We finished about half of it while I was there. After he was shot there was all that interest in him again, so they finally put it out."

Lou had heard about this. It came out a few years ago, but he'd never picked it up. It was called *a*. Warhol thought that would be funny. Nothing on the cover except his name and a single letter.

"He got mad at me because I wouldn't type the bad words."

"What do you mean?"

"It was supposed to be a novel that Andy was 'writing,' but it was just transcriptions of things that happened at the Factory. Conversations. Phone calls. Ondine scoring drugs, Andy talking to Paul Morrissey, and stuff like that. You're even in there."

"Me?"

"Yeah, or else someone just mentioned you, I forget. We changed some of the names, but you could tell who people were. Later on, Paul noticed I was leaving a bunch of blank spots on the pages. The blank spots were where the dirty words should have been. He asked why I wasn't typing what I heard on the tapes and I just told him, 'I don't like that kind of talk.'"

This makes Lou laugh. It's the first genuine thing he's laughed at in weeks.

"Paul begged me to put in at least the first letter, so they could add them in later, but I refused."

"That's so great, Moesy. You're one of a kind."

"That's nothing! There was some stuff I refused to type at all."

In the other room the baby begins to cry. Moe gets up and goes to pick up her daughter.

"Like what?" Lou calls out.

Moe returns, holding the baby. The child's eyes are sleepy and only half-open.

"Oh, there was this whole weird thing."

"What was it?"

"Well, I guess Andy knew some guy who ended up

being a real creep. He was violent. People paid him to beat people up at parties, stuff like that."

Lou can't believe this. It has to be Donato.

"Yeah?" he says. "What else?"

"This guy had an idea to kill someone on camera. A girl, I think. Like, the real thing. He pitched it to Andy as an idea for one of his movies."

The baby begins to drool. Moe grabs a rag that's sitting atop an issue of *TV Guide*. Picking up the rag exposes the smiling face of Mary Tyler Moore.

"When was this?"

She wipes the baby's mouth and nods to the appointment book.

"From around then. December, if not November. Andy used to practically pop out the tapes as soon as they were filled and give them to someone to type. You remember what a production line that place was."

Lou can still see the stacks and stacks of canvases.

"And then there was like a follow up conversation a few weeks later between Andy and Paul. From January, I think. Apparently, the film got made and they were both freaking out. They'd screened it privately a couple of times and people were starting to talk about it. Paul was telling Andy they had to get rid of it, that they should start covering their tracks."

"What did Andy say?"

"Oh, you know Andy. He said it was better than television, that people would love it. That it was a real-life version of one of those death paintings of his. Something like that."

Lou considers all this.

"Anyway," Moe continues, "I think it was all just a joke."

"What was a joke?"

"The tapes. And the film." She turns from the baby and looks at Lou. "Don't you think? I mean, Andy and Paul *knew* they were being recorded. There were cameras and tape recorders all over the Factory. I think they were just trying to create drama. Or freak me out or something. No one would actually *do* something like that, would they?" She bounces the baby. "Either way, it worked. I couldn't bring myself to type a single word of it."

Lou looks to the floor and says, slowly, "What did you do with the tapes?"

She grins.

"I still have them. One of them anyway."

"Really?"

Moe shrugs. "Hell, stuff was going missing from the Factory all the time. Those street kids robbed Andy blind. No one was going to miss one of those cheap cassettes. I know for a fact that one of the other girls who took the tapes home to work on them lost them. Andy had a million things going on back then. He never checked on little things like that."

"Do you still have it? The cassette?"

She grins again.

"I sure do. You wanna hear it?"

Lou nods and Moe gets up, walking with the baby to another part of the house. She returns a minute later with the tape. She looks around the room.

"We got a hi-fi, but no tape player."

Lou stands up.

"I have one, Moe, at home. Can I borrow this?"

She hands it over.

"Sure, but don't lose it. It may be worth something someday."

"Which one is this? Which conversation, I mean?"

Moe looks at the cassette and tries to remember.

"I think the first conversation with the guy. I don't have the one between Paul and Andy."

Lou leans in for a hug.

"Well, I better be going."

"Wait, Lou." Moe turns serious. "I have something I want to tell you."

He sits back down.

"Sure, Moesy, what's up?"

She pauses a second before speaking.

"The band is going to go on. We're staying together."

Lou laughs.

"Without me? How?"

"Doug knows a guy from his old band in Boston. His name's Walter. He's going to play bass and Doug's moving to guitar."

Lou seethes. Doug had been asking to make that change ever since joining the band in '68. He only reluctantly took Cale's spot on bass. Lou figures he'd just been lying low the whole time, waiting for an opportunity like this.

"But, Moe, they're *my* songs."

"Yeah, and you let Doug sing a whole bunch of them. Atlantic sent me the new record the other day." She points to the other room. "Lou, why'd you let him sing so many songs?"

Lou is slowly realizing how easy he made it for his

manager to keep the band going without him. Still, Doug only sang on a handful of tracks. There's no way he can handle "Heroin." No way he can pull off a whole set as the front man.

"There's more," she says.

"Yeah?" Lou replies with a sneer. "What?"

"We're going into the studio in November. Doug has a few songs he wants us to record."

"Is it that piece of shit, 'She'll Make You Cry'?"

After she nods, Lou slaps at his knee. Yule had played the song for him a couple of times at soundcheck, offering it up to be a new song for the band. Lou had listened politely but passed. He's the songwriter in the group.

"And we have some shows," Moe continues. "After the studio."

"Where?"

"Pennsylvania, I think. Bryn Mawr."

Lou takes a few seconds before responding.

"And you're going to do this? Sterling too?"

"I told you not to quit, Lou."

"Jesus, Moe, we didn't have any money! Paul and Andy made ten or twelve thousand bucks for those shows at the Dom, and how much did we get? Five bucks a day. And I didn't want to tour anymore. We were never going to be accepted. Never." He kicks at the bright orange carpet. "At a certain point, you just have to stop."

"Maybe you're right, but I'm not at that point yet."

The baby begins to cry.

"Look at me, Lou. I got a kid. I'm a college dropout. You think I can go back to IBM and be a data puncher? You think *that's* going to make ends meet? I need the money."

Lou's anger begins to soften. He gives a slight laugh.

"Okay, Moesy, if you want to go play ski lodges or something with a fucking Velvet Underground cover band, I'm not going to stop you."

She grins and says, "Watch your language."

He grins too. She's the only person who can talk to him like that.

"Sorry," he says, smiling. He stands up. "Listen, thanks for the tape. You do what you got to do."

She accepts this.

"I will. You too. Okay?"

He leans in for another hug. The baby smells like talcum powder.

"Bye, Moesy."

"Bye, honeybun."

He lets himself out.

●

He wants to listen to the tape right away but, when he gets home, his mom makes him take Seymour for a walk. She's in the kitchen chopping vegetables for dinner while his grandma, wearing the same housecoat and slippers he'd seen her in that morning, is still in the easy chair watching a talk show. Lou takes Seymour to a park by their house near some basketball courts. Growing up, Lou would often play there with his friend Allan. He lets Seymour off the leash and sits on a park bench while his dog chases birds and squirrels.

Lou doesn't know what to be more upset about, that Moe's appointment books hadn't absolved him of

Donato's murder or the fact that she and Sterling are going to try and continue with the Velvet Underground without him. Lou feels like a fool for underestimating his manager. He must have been planning this for a while, if not all along. Lou should have seen it coming but hadn't. He pushes all that out of his head and thinks about Donato.

That Andy was considering capturing a murder on film doesn't surprise Lou. The Factory was an extreme scene—the fact that Warhol had been gunned down and almost killed proved it—but Lou also wants to believe, the same as Moe, that it was just some kind of joke. People were full of shit back then, telling grandiose lies and making up unbelievable backstories. Everyone wanted to impress Andy.

"Okay, Seymour, let's go."

The dog, tongue out and tail wagging, returns and Lou reattaches the leash. He walks home in a daze and puts Seymour in the backyard. His mom is still in the kitchen cooking. The TV is finally off, his grandma taking her afternoon nap.

"Lou, I'm making your favorite."

Crossing the room, he replies, "That's great, Ma."

He goes to his room and locks the door. Lou finds his tape recorder. He's been using it to record songs, including the ones he played that morning.

He put in the cassette Moe gave him, a BASF C-60. Both sides are labeled 11/8/66. He puts in side A, rewinds it to the beginning, and presses Play. He hears opera, footsteps, shuffling paper. Lou can almost make out a conversation between Billy Name and Brigid, but it's soon drowned out by Warhol saying, "What?" right into the microphone. This is followed by a long mono-logue by Ondine about drugs. He ends his speech by say-ing to someone, "Oh, it's the compliment I want to pay to you, my love, was that I know that you are one of the only people I know who do not have to take drugs."

Lou stops the tape and fast-forwards. Pressing Play again he hears Rotten Rita. Rita was a guy named Ken-neth. Some people called him the Mayor. He's saying, "I had a series of warts on my face, and the doctor did each of them with—"

Fast-forward. Ondine again. "Eric was one of the first suicides. I think he was the *first* suicide."

Fast-forward. Nothing but opera.

Fast-forward. Billy Name. "Did you hear what he said to me in the third person?"

When the tape ends, Lou flips it over. He hears Paul Morrissey's voice for the first time, talking to Ondine. "Do you ever go to the movies at all?"

Ondine answers, "The movies I never bother with."

As Lou keeps fast-forwarding and listening, trying to find the discussion between Andy and Donato, Lou hears the Mercedes pull into the garage as the smell of pot roast wafts underneath his door. Dinner will be soon.

Finally, he finds it. There isn't much noise in the back-ground—it must have been either very late or very early—so he can clearly hear the voices. First, Warhol.

"Well, what—I mean, what's wrong with my movies?"

"Edie puking into a toilet, or *pretending* to be stran-gled?" The voice is slow and southern. It has to be Donato. "What kind of fake, make-believe bullshit is that?"

"People, uh, like the movies. Jonas always says—"

"I'm talking about capturing something *real*, Andy. You did all those paintings about death. Why don't you and I make a film about it?"

"Who—what kind of film?"

"A *real* film. Call it *Snuff*. I can be your new superstar."

"Oh, wow, that's fabulous."

"We can capture the whole thing," Donato continues. "The *real* thing. I even know who it could be."

"Who it could be—what?"

"My costar. A girl I just met." Here Donato whispers, even though it sounds like no one else is around. "Nobody will miss her. She's a runaway. I'll even get rid of the body."

As Andy considers this, footsteps can be heard in the background followed by voices. Ondine and Sugar Plum Fairy begin to argue about Obetrol versus Desoxyn.

"Well, let me talk to Paul," Andy finally replies. "He has a basement and maybe we could—"

As the tape runs out, the Play button pops up, causing Lou to jump.

Hearing Donato's voice has unnerved him. It was so slow and calm. Most people who hung around the Factory were on speed. Conversations happened at a mile a minute, a verbal machine-gun assault. But Donato wasn't like that at all. He seemed so serene and spoke so slowly that Lou almost thought the tape recorder was malfunctioning, running at half speed. But he knows it wasn't because Warhol and the others sounded normal.

Lou looks across the room and sees the silver film can. There are some small patches of red rust along the edges and along the top. He puts aside the tape recorder and reaches for the metal container. He considers the yellowing sticker on the top. He figures AWE stands for Andy Warhol Enterprises. The date, 11/19/66, corresponds to the general time period of Moe's tape.

Lou pries open the film can. Inside, a short 16 mm film is wound around a black metal sprocket. Reaching in for the reel, he sees something else. A silver locket, a heart on a long silver chain. Hands again shaking, Lou opens the locket. Inside are two small black-and-white photos, a man and a woman. They seem to be about forty. The man has chunky black glasses and sideburns and the woman has a beehive hairdo that's too big to fit inside the photo. Lou sets this aside.

Grabbing the sprocket, he turns it in his hands and reaches for the foot or so of film that has come unspooled. It's still mostly light outside, so he brings the film to the window. Lou can hear Seymour in the backyard barking at something. Lou holds the film to the light. Each frame is small, about the width of a fingernail. All he can see is some sort of room and a chair. He can tell right away it's not Paul Morrissey's basement. It's a living room, an apartment. Lou is unspooling more film when his mom knocks on the door.

"Lou, time for dinner."

He puts the film back into the can and calls out, "Coming, Ma."

●

Pot roast is usually his favorite. He badgered his mom all the time to make it when he was a kid, but he's not in the mood for it tonight. His mood is contagious. Everyone serves themselves in silence. Lou takes small portions and only pushes the piles around his plate.

"Haven't seen you in the office much this week, Lewis."

His dad tries to say this in a lightweight way, an ice-breaker. But everything he says sounds to his son like a rebuke. Lou doesn't answer. He just shoves peas and carrots around.

"Pass the butter," his grandmother says.

As his mom passes the dish, she keeps her eye on Lou. She doesn't want a fight to ruin another dinner.

"It's just, when I took you on at the firm, I had certain expectations."

Lou's mom closes her eyes. She was hoping her husband would just let it go, but obviously that's not going to happen.

"Sorry, Pops," Lou replies, robotically. "I'd tell you to take it out of my pay, but there's not much of it in the first place."

"When I was your age, Lewis"—Sidney Reed points with his butter knife as he speaks—"I would have been *very* grateful to earn forty dollars a week."

Lou buries his head in his hands. The fork he's holding feels cool against his temple.

"Christ, Dad, that was in the forties. You probably could have bought the Lincoln for that much back then."

His mom chuckles, but quickly adds, "Now, don't be fresh, Son."

Lou touches his mom on the shoulder and says, "Sorry, Ma."

Seymour, who had been sleeping on the rug in the living room, sidles up next to Sidney Reed. Lou's dad smiles and gives the dog a chunk of meat.

"That dog's more a part of this family than I am," Lou says.

"That's because he's here more often than you are," his dad replies.

Lou throws his fork down. It hits his plate and causes a chunk of porcelain to chip off.

Without a word, his grandma picks up her food and walks to the living room. A second later they hear the sound of a helicopter. TV news. Vietnam.

His mom tries to defuse the situation.

"Boys, *please*. Not tonight."

Sidney Reed places a hand on his wife's forearm.

"Toby, it's nothing. We're just having a discussion, that's all."

As his parents take a few more bites, Lou continues to stare at his food.

"I'm just trying to instill a work ethic in Lewis, the same way my dad did in me. He owned his own business, and now I own my own business. It'd be a shame for that to go to waste. The firm is doing so well."

"Dad, I don't want to inherit the business."

"Son, you have a flair. You're a good typist. You could learn, maybe even go back to school and—"

"Bunny, Dad. Bunny's the one you need to give the firm to, not me. She has a better head for those things." Lou picks up a roll and quickly puts it down. "She's the kind of child you could be proud of."

"Merrill wants other things, Lewis."

"And what about what I want, Pops?"

"I would say you've had plenty of time to indulge in

all the things *you* want." Sidney Reed spoons a forkful of vegetables into his mouth. "It's time you forgot about that and became more responsible."

Under his breath, Lou says, "I know I disappointed you, Mom. I know you feel that way too, Dad."

"No, dear," his mom pleads. "That's not true. We just—"

"I'm not married, and there's no grandson on the way," he continues, cutting her off. "I know you both resent the life I've led. Warhol and rock and roll. New York City and all of that. But I just didn't want anything you want."

"Come on, let's not start this business again," Sidney Reed says. "We're a family, Lewis. We welcomed you home with open arms, and we're glad to have you here."

His mom nods, holding back tears.

"Dad, we don't have anything in common anymore except . . . our name."

Something in his father seems to break. His placid demeanor suddenly gives way to rage. "Why, you spiteful little bastard," his dad says with anger, "we gave you everything."

"You never gave me shit."

"Lewis," his mom says, her voice strained, "I'm *begging* you."

"Yeah, you both did a great job," Lou continues, undeterred, "you and your two-bit psychiatrists."

"Don't you bring that up again." Sidney Reed had raised his napkin to wipe his mouth, but instead he balls it up and throws it onto the table. "That's your excuse for everything."

"I can't remember things, Dad. Good things. Bad

things. Do you know what it's like to not know who you are? To not know what you've done?"

"The doctors said . . . ," his mom begins, but then stops.

"We only wanted what's best for you, Son. I'm not say-ing we didn't make mistakes. And I know that's hard for you to understand. I only hope that when you have kids, you'll know what it's like." Sidney Reed raises his eyes to his son. "We did our best."

"That's a load of horseshit, Pops."

Lou swipes at his plate, causing it to knock over water glasses and dishes. An upended gravy boat makes a stain on the white tablecloth like what he saw on Donato's rug. He goes to his room and slams the door.

As he sits on his bed, he can hear the sobs of his mom from the dining room. His dad's voice, trying to calm her, is shaky. He must be crying too. Lou blames Long Island. Freeport had done this to them. He could not remember anything bad happening in Brooklyn.

FRIDAY

THE MORNING DRIVE to the office is tense. Sidney Reed doesn't say anything, and Lou just sits and stares out the window, the silver film can on his lap. He shouldn't have gone to the office at all—he's planning to head to Manhattan as soon as he can. He has his meeting at Atlantic at noon, and before that he has a friend he's hoping can run Donato's reel. Lou only went with his dad because he didn't want to make any calls about the film at home. His mom and his grandma would be around, and they'd overhear.

At the office, the girls all look at Lou skeptically. Like his father, they'd noticed how much work he'd missed this week. Lou doesn't care. This is all temporary. He's just getting back on his feet, but they'll be here forever.

Sitting down, he sees his desk is covered with mail to be sorted and letters that need to be typed. He pushes it all aside, sets down the film can, and reaches for the telephone. He picks up the receiver with one hand and fishes in his pocket with the other. He pulls out the number he'd found in his notebook. It's early, so he's hoping to catch Jonas at home.

He met Jonas Mekas around the same time the band

first came in contact with Warhol. Mekas was part of Manhattan's underground film scene. He and Barbara Rubin filmed the Velvet Underground's performance at a psychiatrist's convention in '66. Even back then, he'd been part of Warhol's scene for years. Jonas had premiered Andy's five-and-a-half-hour movie *Sleep* at the beginning of '64. Nine people were in the audience, and two left in the first hour. As part of a collective called the Film-Makers' Cinematheque, Mekas showed experimental art films all over town. Up at the Jewish Museum at Ninety-Second and Fifth, at the Elgin at Eighth Avenue, and in midtown on West Forty-First.

As the number rings, Lou drums his fingers on the film can. All he brought was the reel. The silver locket is in a drawer in his room. When the phone rings for the sixth time, Lou's sure he's called too late, that Jonas has already left for the day. But then someone picks up.

"Hello?"

"Jonas, hey, it's Lou. How ya doing?"

"Lou! You barely caught me. I was just heading out ze door."

Jonas, born in Lithuania, sounds just like Lou's grandmother.

"Far out, Jonas. Hey, look, I have some kind of film here I got through a friend of Andy's. It's a short, just one reel. Could you help me see it? Screen it or whatever?"

While Jonas is considering this, Lou watches as Ray arrives and starts handing out the coffee orders. His first delivery is to Jeanie, who complains about having milk in her coffee instead of cream.

"Sure, Lou. I'll be downtown," Jonas finally answers.

"We're getting ready to open our new place in November but, for you, I will do favor."

"Out of sight, Jonas, thanks."

He grabs a pencil, writes down the address on a piece of company stationery, and tells Mekas he'll be there about eleven. Just to get his dad off his back, Lou spends an hour doing work. He figures the mail can wait, opting instead to tackle all the letters that are on his desk. He types like a madman, finishes them all, and slips out of the office.

The address Jonas gave him turns out to be the Public Theater on Lafayette, around the corner from Cooper Union and just up from the Bowery. Lou knows the building from when he first moved to New York. Back then it was empty and run-down, vacant and decaying. But the city has since begun to realize that history is worth preserving and that not every old building should be bulldozed to make way for a tower of plastic and glass. This building was one of the first to be spared. Today, its arched windows are freshly painted, and its grand red-brick and terra cotta facade shines.

Lou finds Jonas in a small lobby just off the main theater entrance. Mekas is looking over a list on a clipboard. He's surrounded by stacks of boxes, rolled-up film posters, and silver film canisters piled taller than he is. His thinning hair is gray at the temples and his brown suit is rumpled. He resembles the college professors at Syracuse Lou had never paid much attention to.

"Jonas, hey."

He turns and gives a big smile.

"My old friend, how are you?"

"Can't complain." Lou points to all the stuff strewn about the lobby. "What is all this?"

Jonas smiles even wider.

"I finally have my own theater. Me and my colleagues are curating a collection of essential films. The entire history of cinema will be under one roof!"

After reminiscing for a few minutes, Lou hands him the film can. Jonas examines the label. He'd seen it plenty of times before.

"This is a Warhol?" He pronounces Andy's last name as *Varhall*.

Lou shrugs.

"I don't exactly know what it is. That's why I brought it to you."

"Okay, follow me."

Jonas leads Lou to the theater. At almost 150 seats, it's bigger than the basements and living rooms where Mekas has shown his avant-garde movies in years past. Even though there are drop cloths and scaffolding in the corner, and the entire room is filled with the smell of paint, it looks like a proper movie theater.

"I go to projection booth," Jonas says. "Give me few minutes and I run your movie like I did Andy's movies."

Lou takes an aisle seat four rows from the front. He feels strange being in such a big theater all by himself. He's only seen movies as part of a crowd. Even in the world of underground films, there's usually a few other people there, even if they're just passing a joint and not watching the film.

After the lights go out and Lou waits for the film to start, he realizes that the screen isn't white, it's gray. Almost silver. This reminds him of the first Factory, with its tinfoil walls and gallons of silver paint. By the time Lou arrived on the scene, Warhol had mostly retired from painting. His breakthrough years of the soup cans, Coke bottles, and silver Elvises were behind him. And while he still produced work, it was gimmicky stuff like the cow wallpaper. Out of ideas, he turned to film. Whether that meant the short screen tests Andy made visitors sit for, or the marathon cinematic experiences like *Empire* and *Sleep*, there were always cameras and Paul Morrissey and Andy were always working on a movie. The same as Jonas, they wanted their work to be shown in places other than a basement in the Village or a loading dock in Brooklyn. They dreamt of the big time. Hollywood. It was unlikely they'd get there with eight-hour films about buildings but, nevertheless, it was something they always talked about.

Lou was never in any of the movies. He'd stayed away from all that. There were a lot of things at the Factory he stayed away from. Edie and the superstars just seemed to be trouble. He liked Billy Name, and Brigid, but that's about it. The rest were just desperate runaways, and Lou felt he had nothing in common with them. He'd already run away.

The room suddenly lights up white and Lou can hear the whirring of the projector in the booth behind him. There's a test pattern, a counting down of numbers, punched holes in the negative, and then a picture appears. It's the apartment Lou had seen the day before when he'd held the strip of film up to the light. The room's awash in what seems like natural light. A curtain at the edge of the frame moves back and forth slowly, suggesting an open window. He's seen plenty of other Warhol movies, so he knows this isn't either Paul Morrissey's basement or a corner of the Factory.

In the center of the room is an old chair, an antique. It almost looks like a throne. It seems to Lou vaguely familiar. When he notices other things in the room—the arm of a couch, an end table, the corner of a shag rug—Lou suddenly remembers. The storage space. This is all of Donato's stuff. Lou assumes that what he's seeing is Donato's apartment.

After a minute of the film being just the chair and the gently swaying curtains, Donato enters the frame. Having only seen him in photos, it gives Lou the chills to see the dead man move. For a big guy, he seems to have a light step. Lou figures this is a skill he learned in the military. If an enemy hears you coming, you're dead already. But there's something else. The movie is the opposite of those old flickering silent films where everyone walks in double time and every movement is exaggerated and fast. When Donato walks—he's again wearing a fashionable tie and what looks to be an expensive suit—the tie moves back and forth in a slow, dreamy motion. Donato himself appears to float.

He walks behind the chair, smiling and talking to someone out of frame. There's no sound, but the look on Donato's face—along with his body language—suggests he's trying to get someone to join him. He keeps talking and pointing at the chair. It isn't working, and Donato appears to become frustrated. He finally walks out of frame, reentering a few seconds later firmly holding the upper arm of a young woman. He seats her in the chair and points to the camera. Donato motions to the girl to smile. She doesn't smile.

Even though the film's in black and white, Lou can tell she's a blonde. Pretty, but not a knockout. She has big eyes and a small nose. Her mouth is slightly open, as if she wants to say something but is too scared to do so. She's dressed conservatively in a short dress and Mary Janes. As she sits there, looking awkward and self-conscious, a piece of her jewelry catches the afternoon light. A silver locket, shaped like a heart. Lou recognizes it as the one he found in the film can.

The girl begins to grip the arms of the chair, appearing to want to stand up—maybe even to leave—but Donato attempts to soothe her by running his huge hands over first her shoulders and then her neck. The girl startles, cringing at his touch, but soon begins to relax. The way her head lolls, and her legs are splayed, makes Lou think she's been drugged. As Donato strokes the girl's neck, he slowly turns to the camera. He grins as his fingers close in and press on the young girl's flesh.

When she realizes what's happening, she tries to get up, but Donato's size and power are too much for her. He pushes her down and continues to squeeze the girl's neck while leering into the camera. She starts to panic, clawing at the chair and uselessly kicking her legs. Donato just keeps on squeezing, his face turning into a more and more grotesque mask the harder the girl struggles to stay alive.

Lou can hear, in the projection booth, Jonas say, "Jesus, no."

On the huge screen, Donato continues to strangle the girl. As her life slowly drains out, one of her hands reaches up and back—to try and stop him—but her arm only makes it a few inches before it flops down. Her eyes finally close, her body stops moving, and her tongue flops out of her mouth. A puddle of drool falls on the front of her dress. Donato's breathing heavily, still staring into the camera. His leer has transformed into something like ecstasy. He stands there, relishing the moment, before finally standing up straight, smoothing his hair, adjusting his tie, and walking slowly out of frame. Lou notices one of the girl's shoes came off in the struggle. Her toes are painted something dark, probably red.

The film continues for what feels like a long time, the light in the room changing as the New York sunshine shifts with the clouds. The dead girl's hair occasionally floats on a breeze from the open window. It looks a lot like Andy's movie *Sleep*, except it's more than that.

When the movie finally ends, the screen going suddenly black, Lou jumps. Jonas turns on the lights and joins him in the theater.

"That was real, no?"

Lou gets up and says, "Yes, but it was so . . . slow."

"Films are shot at twenty-four frames per second," Mekas says. "I did what Warhol always wants and projected it at sixteen frames. Everything is slowed down, like a dream. Even death."

"Thanks, Jonas. Sorry if I ruined your morning."

They shake hands and Jonas returns to the projection booth.

Lou walks up the aisle and out of the theater. As he makes his way through the lobby, Jonas comes running after him with the film can.

"Lou, take this. I don't want."

Lou stops and raises his hands. He doesn't want the film either.

"Can't you just lose it somewhere? Stick it in the back of a filing cabinet?" Lou waves his arm around the crowded lobby. It resembles the last scene in *Citizen Kane*, the huge warehouse filled with things. "Or can't you just put it in with all this other stuff? No one would ever find it."

Jonas shakes his head and smiles.

"Lou, in World War II I was. Saw many horrible things. My brother and I spent a year in a forced labor camp in Germany. I have seen enough death. I'm done with all that. This is why I like the movies." He hands Lou the film can. "Film isn't real."

Lou takes the metal container, thanks his friend again, and steps out onto Lafayette.

●

Lou walks up the street in a daze, the film can in his hand feeling like a weight. He can't get the face of the dead girl out of his mind. He keeps replaying the moment the light slowly went out of her eyes, and how Donato had just grinned and leered into the camera. As he crosses Saint Marks Place, Lou remembers the name in the address book that had the line through it. Kathy. That must be the girl. Knowing her name makes it worse.

So many people drifted through the scene back then, but Lou never knew who anyone was. He'd see a face at the Factory, or in the back room of Max's, and weeks later he might hear how they skipped town, overdosed, or joined a commune. People became anecdotes, stories to pass the time. The fact that everyone had colorful nicknames made it all seem like a fantasy. Ultra Violet, Sugar Plum Fairy, Cherry Vanilla. They were characters, not people. But Lou could now picture the dead girl as a person with a past and a future that would never arrive. He'd once seen a man beaten to death in an after-hours club but, while that had been disturbing, it was nothing like this. He hadn't known the guy, and didn't know what the circumstances were (at the time, all Lou could think of was that maybe the guy deserved it). This is different. It's cold-blooded murder, and Donato enjoyed it.

Feeling the weight of the film can in his hand makes him think of the storage space. Lou looks at his watch. It's not yet eleven. He has more than an hour before he's due to meet Danny Fields at the Atlantic offices uptown. Lou decides to pay another visit to Donato's things. Maybe he missed something. Maybe one of those other pieces of furniture also holds a secret compartment, and he'll find more mementos from the sailor's adventures in the city.

Lou makes a quick stop at Stromboli's for two slices of cheese pizza and a Coke. Then he hails a cab to Twenty-Third Street. Entering the office of the storage facility, he sees the same old man from the other day behind the desk. When he recognizes Lou, he slowly gets up. The lockbox with the cards and keys is already on the counter.

"Ah, Mr. Reed," the old man says as he walks slowly to the counter. "You're here to help?"

"Help with what?"

"Why, your associate."

The old man points to the sign-in sheet. Lou puts down the can of film and grabs the clipboard. He can't read the name, but he sees the number: 919.

"What? Who is it?"

"A man. He works at your firm. Said you'd sent him to get some files."

"And you gave him a key?"

The old man's face begins to turn red.

"Why, yes, is there a problem?"

"What else did he say?"

"He—he went up first to see if what he wanted was there. Then he came back down and asked for the key to the freight elevator."

Lou runs through the door in the side of the office. At the end of the long hallway of storage spaces, where he'd seen the freight elevator the other day, there's a huge empty space.

He takes the regular elevator to the ninth floor. From even the end of the hallway he can see the painting. The door to the storage space is open, and the Warhol is being carried to the freight elevator. Lou spots a tuft of black hair above the canvas and a pair of dingy sneakers below it.

Lou yells, "Stop!" and runs down the hallway. Whoever's carrying the Warhol drops it and dashes for the freight elevator. Lou reaches the elevator just as the huge doors are pulled shut from the inside. A light inside comes on and the elevator begins to descend. Lou quickly puts the painting back in the space, locks it, and sprints back to the regular elevator.

As the doors open on the first floor, Lou darts into the hallway. The freight elevator's not there yet. As Lou approaches the empty space, the freight elevator slowly arrives. He's raising his fists when the doors open in a flash and he's struck with two sharp blows to the face and one to the gut. The punches cause Lou to fall to the floor in a heap. As he tries to regain his breath, he hears foot-steps run down the hallway and through the door to the office.

Standing up, Lou tastes blood. One of the punches split his lip and the other caught him right in the eye. A bruise is already beginning to form. He figures that who-ever hit him is already in a cab, blocks away.

When Lou walks back into the office, the old man is standing at the counter. Seeing the state that Lou is in, he says with fascination, "I had no idea accounting was such a dangerous profession."

•

By the time he arrives at Atlantic Records, his lip is still bleeding. When he asks the young receptionist for a tis-sue, she hands one over reluctantly and waves him toward a group of chairs arrayed around a glass-and-chrome cof-fee table. Lou decides to stand, holding the can of film and wandering around the spacious lobby. There are huge black-and-white portraits of Aretha Franklin, Led Zep-pelin, Dusty Springfield, Cream, and a dozen other per-formers who'd had hits for Atlantic. Lou and the band only signed to the label in March. He doesn't feel like he's part of the Atlantic family, and he certainly doesn't have anything in common with the acts enshrined on the wall. And now that he's quit the band, he figures this will prob-ably be the last time he'll ever come here.

"Lou!"

He turns to see Danny Fields walking across the lobby. They embrace in a hug.

Danny has long hair and almost translucent bright blue eyes. He's from Brooklyn. Lou likes that; it's something they have in common.

"Come on back."

Danny leads Lou through a labyrinth of offices, cubicles, and conference rooms. On the walls are more framed photos of bands and musicians. Lou looks for a picture of the Velvet Underground but doesn't see one. They finally reach Danny's office.

As they both sit down—Danny in a large leather chair behind a steel desk and Lou in a small black metal chair in front of the desk—Danny points to Lou's battered face.

"You rock stars really like to live dangerously, don't you?"

Lou puts the tissue again to his face—his lip seems to have finally stopped bleeding. The coppery taste is gone.

"One of my rabid fans."

Danny laughs. The Velvet Underground had never been particularly popular. They mostly played clubs or small rooms. For that last run of shows at Max's, even though they were in their hometown, it was half-empty most nights.

"What do you have there?" Danny points at the silver can of film.

"Death," Lou answers. "You know, the usual."

Danny laughs again.

"Seen Nico lately?"

"No, you?"

Danny nods.

"Saw her play a few months ago. You should *see* her, Lou. She just stands there and plays this wheezing box. It sounds like a fucking bagpipe or something. You should help her."

Back when Paul Morrissey co-managed the Velvet Underground with Warhol, he got Nico small shows in basements and coffeehouses. It wasn't much, but she had a young son and needed to earn money. Musicians like Tim Buckley, Tim Hardin, and Jackson Browne would accompany her on acoustic guitar. Lou even backed her for a couple of shows.

"I heard she and John are making another record in London."

Danny nods again.

"They *are*, Lou. John's becoming a great producer. Did you hear that Stooges album?"

Lou sulks in the metal chair. He'd pushed Cale out of the group after just two records and had done everything he could to reduce Nico's role, all but ensuring she wasn't around after the LP they did with Andy. Now John's producing bands and putting out solo albums, and Nico's finishing her third record. Lou feels left behind.

"Danny, I want to talk about the album."

Danny frowns, as if he'd hoped this was more of a social call than a business meeting. They hadn't seen each other since that last show at Max's.

"What's the problem *now*, Lou?"

"I got the record this week. 'Sweet Jane' and 'New Age' have been butchered. There's a minute missing from the end of 'New Age,' and the bridge in 'Sweet Jane' has been totally axed. I worked for a year on those songs, and you ruined them."

As Lou's talking, Danny gets up and flips through a rack of records sitting atop a filing cabinet. These are all of Atlantic's recent releases. Danny's job is to get publicity for the label's larger acts. He pulls out a copy of *Loaded*.

"Lou, I thought you *agreed* to those edits. To get them on the radio. That's why you came to us, right? To get hits?"

Lou grabs the album. Danny sighs and sits down.

"Well then, what the hell is this artwork supposed to mean?"

The sleeve's an illustration of a subway entrance, pink vapor hovering over the stairs.

"I don't know," Danny says. "The 'underground,' I guess?"

"A bit literal, don't you think?"

"I know it's not great, but that artist has done a bunch of covers for us, Lou. He even did a sleeve for Ornette Coleman. You *love* Ornette Coleman."

"Yeah, well, I don't love this. Look"—Lou points to the sign above the stairs—"the fucker even misspelled 'downtown.' How hard is that to get right?"

As Danny twists his head to see, he says, "Well, he's Polish. His English is not so good."

Lou turns over the sleeve. The back is what had made his blood boil when he saw the record earlier in the week. At the top is a large black-and-white photo of the studio where the album was recorded. It's in the same building as the Atlantic offices, just a few floors away from where he is now. The picture, taken from inside the control room, shows baffles, amps, microphones, drums. On the far right, sitting at the piano, is Doug Yule. Below the photo are the album's credits.

"What's with this picture?"

"What's wrong with it?"

Lou flashes it to Danny.

"What, did the photographer show up when I wasn't around? Was he waiting for me to leave the room or something?"

"Lou, I don't see why that's bad."

"Danny, this makes it look like Doug's the mastermind behind the record."

Fields says slowly, "Oh, I don't know about *that*." Danny had been part of the Factory scene almost from the beginning, and he'd taken to mimicking Warhol's laconic way of speaking.

"And look at this." Lou points to where it says THE LINE UP. "It lists the band, with Doug first. Then Sterl, then me, and then Moe. And look at all the instruments it has Doug playing. Eight. Eight goddamn instruments, like he's a musical genius or something. And what's this shit? 'Lyrics and song composition.' Tell me, Danny, what songs did Doug compose exactly?"

"I don't know, Lou. You tell *me*."

Lou waves toward the hallway, where workers are already starting to leave for the day, getting a jump on the weekend.

"Can you ask somebody, then? I'd like to know what songs Doug composed." Lou points again to the sleeve. "For Sterling it even says that too. 'Song composition.' That's bullshit."

Danny stands up and tries to take the record from Lou. Lou doesn't let him.

"And look at this," he continues, "the songs are all out of order. I had a sequence, and you ruined it."

He points to the bottom, where it says *All selections are by The Velvet Underground.*

"So then, we *all* wrote these songs? That's not true, and you know it. I wrote everything on this record. I can prove it. In fact, I'm going to—"

Danny raises his hands to get his friend to stop talking.

"Lou, what do you *want* me to do?"

Lou tosses the album onto the desk.

"I want you to fix this."

"How, Lou? You want me to recall it, change the sleeve? It'd take *months*. That's what killed your first record, remember? Don't let it kill this one too."

"Well, then, how about a single? What's happening with that?"

Danny laughs.

"Why do you want to have a single from the record if you hate the record?"

"It's a year's worth of work, I told you. I don't want it to just . . . disappear."

Danny looks at the schedule of releases on his desk and runs his finger down some columns.

"Six months, maybe. But nothing before then."

Lou gets up and paces around the small office. Danny has a view of Columbus Circle and the southwest edge of Central Park just beyond. Lou can see hansom cabs giving rides to tourists.

"Lou, I told you when I brought you to the label, I can't have a personal and professional relationship with you at the same *time*."

"I know, Danny. I know."

"You also know what a fan I am of the band. I *adore* you guys. Don't forget I gave you your first national publicity."

This was back in '66 when Danny was working at a teen magazine called *Datebook*. While he was there he managed to get coverage for groups he liked. Seeing Iggy Pop next to David Cassidy or the Doors next to the Monkees must have been a jarring experience for suburban teenyboppers. This was also when Danny got the Beatles in trouble by reprinting an old interview where they compared themselves to Jesus.

Lou sits down in a huff and points to the Cotillion logo.

"And why do we have to be on an imprint? Why can't we just be on Atlantic?" Lou grabs the list of releases from Danny's desk. Seeing the names of the other Cotillion artists makes him bite his lip and taste blood again. "Rusty Kershaw, the Marbles, Edison Electric Band . . . Who the fuck are these people?"

"Look, Cotillion's the blues and southern soul imprint. *Someone* has to put out that stuff."

"Yeah, but why are *we* on it? Jesus, Danny, what did you get me involved in here?"

Danny, beginning to lose patience, takes a deep breath before speaking.

"I got you *signed*, Lou. You weren't exactly a hot property, remember? You fired Warhol, your records never sold, and you guys were only ever popular in Boston and New York."

"That's not true, Danny. We got good crowds in Philadelphia, and at the Matrix out in San Francisco. Plus there was La Cave in Cleveland. They loved us in Cleveland."

Danny rolls his eyes.

"Ohio doesn't count, and you know it."

"I'm serious, Danny. What are you going to do for us?" Lou points again to the hallway, to the warren of offices and cubicles. "What are you going to make them do for us?"

"Lou, you left the band! There's nothing else *to* do. We're going to get it into the shops, maybe place a couple of ads, but that's it."

Lou pounds a fist on the corner of the desk.

"We have a contract. We owe you another record."

Danny considers this. On the street below there's a burst of noise. Cars honking and an ambulance.

"I saw Brigid the night of your last show. She told me she taped it. Maybe we could—"

"Nah," Lou waves away the idea. "I heard the tapes the other day. They're garbage. No one will want to listen to that shit."

Danny's phone rings. He looks relieved.

"Lou, I have to take this call. I'll see what I can do, okay?"

Lou grabs the can of film and stands up. He feels drained. All he can think of to say is "Okay."

●

Lou leaves Atlantic and starts walking south toward Penn Station. He crosses Forty-Eighth and catches the light at Forty-Seventh. A dozen blocks to go. The film canister in his hand feels like a dumbbell and he's hot from his argument with Danny. His head's also still throbbing from the punches he'd taken at the storage facility. Lou can feel a shiner growing under the bruised flesh of his cheek. Too tired to walk all the way, he stops and hails a taxi.

A cab stops and Lou gets in. It was one of the newer models, with a shiny red-and-black United Taxi Owners Guild sticker on the hood. Rather than head directly back to Freeport, Lou decides to make one more stop. He tells the driver, "Forty-Second and Fifth."

The taxi makes good time down Ninth Avenue but crawls after it makes a left onto Forty-Fourth. As the cab inches its way through Times Square, Lou leans forward and looks around. He loves the depravity of Times Square. This is truly the seedy heart of the city. There are prostitutes and drug dealers everywhere, even though it's the middle of the day. The 25¢ peep shows that led the way for the porn theaters and strip clubs line the streets. Guys with their shirts open to the waist stand outside brothels, enticing customers to enter. A cop sits in his patrol car while a hooker sits on the hood wearing a translucent top.

As the cab crosses Broadway, Lou turns his head and can even see the glowing orange neon of the Howard Johnson's on Forty-Sixth. Outside the Globe Theatre, whose huge marquee boasts THE FILTHIEST SHOW IN TOWN, an old man in a tattered brown suit marches in circles carrying a hand-scrawled sign that reads JESUS SAID SEARCH THE SCRIPTURE. He's losing the battle. That's not what people search for, or find, in Times Square.

A few minutes later, Lou arrives at his destination. He gives the driver two dollars, tells him to keep the change, and gets out of the taxi.

The main branch of the New York Public Library is a

huge and stately building, with three grand arches and a half-dozen Greek columns stretching two stories tall. A pair of lions on pedestals sit in between the steps leading up to the entrance. Students entering and leaving the library mix with sightseers, families, and businessmen who are passing by. Kids lick ice-cream cones and munch huge salted pretzels they'd bought from vendors in Bryant Park, which sits directly behind the library.

Lou had come here once as a child with his father when they were on an errand to the city. His mother and sister had stayed behind in Brooklyn. This was before the big move that ruined everything. Lou can't remember anything about the day's assignment—what they were in the city to do—all he can remember is that they came to this grand, old building. They weren't looking for anything specific, and they didn't leave with an armful of books (though they could have—Lou had a library card, even if his father didn't). Sidney Reed just wanted to show his son the building. Wanted Lou to be impressed by its long rows of wooden tables and the painted mural on the majestic ceiling. Wanted him to be struck by the seriousness of the place, its quiet grandeur and its twin sense of history and knowledge. He wanted his son to know that if he worked hard enough—studied, applied himself, showed real grit—something of his may one day end up here. Even though Lou had scoffed when his dad brought it up, the place had certainly wowed him. And now, entering it as an adult, it does so again.

He steps inside and walks up the marble steps to the second floor. He finds an information booth sitting at the very edge of the reading room. The place is silent. All you can hear is the traffic outside and the faint hum of the desk lamps.

"Yes, how can I help you?"

She's a young blonde in a blue dress. She reminds Lou of the "star" of Donato's movie. He pushes the thought out of his mind and hides the film can behind his back.

"Yeah, I'd like some books on copyright."

"Any particular area?"

"Music," Lou answers. "Songs."

SATURDAY

L OU'S NEVER BEEN to the office on a weekend. Maybe once or twice as a teenager he'd run in to get a file or fetch his father when Sidney Reed was putting in extra hours against a big deadline, but otherwise Lou's only been here during the workweek. As he now walks among the silent desks and dormant typewriters, he decides he likes it better this way. No gossip, no backstabbing, no chitchat. No people. Even the street outside is quiet. It's a sunny day, temperatures are already in the seventies, may even hit eighty. Everyone's at the beach.

Lou walks to his desk and sets down the forms and book he got at the library the day before. The book is huge. *Sound Recordings and Phonorecords: History and Current Law.* He glanced through it at the library and then again at home, dog-earing a number of pages. More important are the dozen copyright forms. Filling them out, and sending them in, will be the first step toward getting back the rights to his songs. No matter what it says on the back of *Loaded*, Lou knows that he wrote those songs. They belong to him.

He grabs the first copyright form and winds it into the typewriter. It's two-sided, with nine sections to fill out.

Four on the front and five on the back. The info to be entered is basic. Title of the work, name of the author, year in which creation of the work was completed, and so on. Lou's going to fill one out for each of the ten songs on the final Velvet Underground record.

As he starts on the first form, for opening track "Who Loves the Sun," Lou realizes this won't be the only thing he'll have to do. At some point, he'll have to confront the band's manager. There might even be a lawsuit.

Ever since that first bad deal he signed with Pickwick in '65—he'd barely looked over the agreement—he's been loath to deal with contracts, lawyers, or managers. He'd even strung along Warhol for months before signing anything, wary of getting stuck in another bad situation. And that was when Andy was at the height of his fame. He'd been on the cover of *Time*, he was everywhere you looked, but that wasn't good enough for Lou. It drove Paul Morrissey crazy.

As Lou flips over the form and begins filling out the back (more basic questions like where to send the certificate—he enters his parents' address), he tries to set in his mind some parameters for the fight he knows is ahead. How far is he willing to go? Should he preemptively sue? Should he just schedule a meeting with his manager and see what happens? The fact that Sterling and Moe are going to continue with the group doesn't give him much leverage. Sure, he wrote the songs, but anyone could sing them. In a dark bar, maybe no one would know the difference.

In anger, Lou rips the finished form from the typewriter. The paper tears in half.

"Goddamnit."

Lou balls up both pieces and tosses them onto the desk. He gets another form and starts over. When he's finished, he moves on to the next song. TITLE OF WORK. "Sweet Jane." NAME OF THE AUTHOR. He grins as he types LOU REED. As he fills in the rest of the boxes, he begins to hum and whisper the lyrics about the song's characters, Jack and Jane.

This makes him think of Sarah from earlier in the week. Is she Sally Mae from "Foggy Notion"? And what about Donato's address book, which holds the names of other people from his songs? Had everything he sang about really happened? He prides himself on being an acute observer, noticing all the little details in a room or on a person. Everything is fodder, everything can go into a song. But he always assumed that what was around him only provided the inspiration for his later creations. He never would have guessed he was just a reporter.

He finishes the form and moves on to the next. He knows "Rock & Roll" is made-up because it's about him. Rock and roll saved his life. Hearing disc jockeys like Murray the K and Alan Freed let him know there was a world beyond Freeport. The radio became a portal to other experiences, a way out of his humdrum existence. You can go anywhere in a song. And the fact that people made money doing it—Elvis had so many cars, he just gave them away—showed there might be a future for him as something other than just an accountant.

Lou pulls out the completed form and reaches for a blank one. He knocks out the rest in a half hour. After placing all ten in a neat stack on top of his desk, he notices the balled-up bits from the one he'd accidentally ripped in half. He grabs the crumpled-up paper and tosses it into a metal wastebasket under his desk. The torn paper lands on something. An envelope and what looks like a letter. Ray's supposed to empty the trash cans each night, but half the time he leaves it for the next morning.

The day before, Lou had only typed letters that were already on his desk. He hasn't gone through the mail in days, the towering stacks are proof. On Friday he'd only been in the office for an hour or so and, in that time, didn't throw anything away. He's sure of it. The trash can should have been empty.

Lou reaches into the wastebasket and pulls out the envelope and letter, instantly recognizing the thin paper. It's from the law firm, the one inquiring about Donato's stuff.

We kindly ask that you respond to our numerous requests regarding the estate of Mr. Samuel Donato. Our client is eager to take quick and final possession of Mr. Donato's things and, if you will not provide them in a timely manner, we will be forced to enter into litigation to compel you to do so.

The mention of "numerous" letters makes Lou realize the one he'd seen on Monday isn't the only one that's been sent. There hadn't been any others in the Donato file, but maybe that's because they'd just been thrown away, same as this one. As a strategy, stonewalling the law firm isn't working since it seems they're ready to take things to the next level. Lou even wonders if his dad had sent out that cockamamie response about Donato being audited. That's not going to work either.

Whoever's behind the push for Donato's things is getting impatient. Lou also wonders if this renewed effort is tied to whoever hit him the day before at the storage facility. Maybe the word is out that Donato's heir has finally shown up and wants the Warhol, and someone else is determined to get to it first.

Lou turns to the large pile of mail. Even though it seems someone has already gone through it—perhaps looking specifically for anything related to the Sailor— Lou wants to search through it again. Maybe there's another letter, something they missed, another clue.

Looking up at the clock, he sees that it's just past noon. Even though he'd had a big breakfast, Lou's starting to feel hungry. He weighs his options, thinking about the rest of his day. He's meeting his parents at the club for dinner. His grandma's going to stay at home, but his sister's passing through town with some med school friends and will join them. She'd called the night before and Lou had persuaded her to get dropped off early, so they can play tennis. She adores Lou—has ever since she was a baby—so naturally she said yes. Lou figures he'll check the stacks of mail and then take a break for lunch.

He grabs the heavy silver letter opener. Before reaching into one of the piles of mail for an envelope, he notices something about the opener. Engraved into the handle are two letters, along with some sort of insignia. The symbol's an anchor with sharp points and a rope looped through a hole at the top. The letters are an *S* and a *D*. Lou thinks about this, trying to place them in the context of the insignia. When it hits him, he throws the letter opener down in shock. It clatters on the cool metal tabletop. S. D. The Sailor. Samuel Donato. The dead man.

"Good morning, Lewis."

Lou looks up, startled.

Sheldon Mayer stands in front of Lou's desk with a curious look on his face. He's dressed the way he always dresses for the office except, because it's the weekend, he skipped the tie. Lou almost doesn't recognize him without it.

After composing himself, Lou answers, "*Afternoon*, Sheldon. Look at the clock. It's now the *afternoon*."

Sheldon Mayer looks at the office clock and grimaces slightly.

"No matter what time it is, Lewis, I certainly didn't expect to see you here on a *Saturday*."

The way he pronounces the word makes him think Sheldon never expects to see Lou on a Monday, Tuesday, Wednesday, Thursday, or Friday either.

"I just had some stuff I wanted to catch up on." Lou points to the stacks of mail. "It's been, you know, a busy week."

Sheldon nods approvingly, adjusts his glasses, and walks across the office to his desk. Lou turns again to the letter opener. He tries to think back, to see if he can remember using it during one of his brief stints helping out his dad in the past. Nothing comes to mind. He never liked coming here, and one letter opener amid a whole room full of supplies wasn't going to stick in his brain. All he can remember is that it's been in the desk ever since he started working here earlier in the month.

Lou wants to go into his dad's office and check Donato's file again. Maybe the letter opener is listed among the Sailor's possessions. Maybe it's an antique and worth something. He glances across the office. Sheldon's sitting at his desk, hunched over a mound of paperwork.

He knows Sheldon will question him if he goes searching for something in his dad's office. Lou's still hazy from yesterday's beating and doesn't think he can come up with a convincing story. He looks at the clock again: 12:22. Lou could try and wait, sticking around until Sheldon leaves, but Lou knows what a kiss-ass he is. Now that the boss's son has seen him come in on a Saturday, Sheldon will probably stay there until Sunday. Lou decides to just come in early next week and try to get a peek at the file then. And since he doesn't want the latest letter from the law firm to get thrown away, he slips it into his back pocket, along with the letter opener.

Lou decides everything else can also wait until next week. He pushes aside all the unopened envelopes, gets up and heads for the door. He's just about to leave when Sheldon calls after him.

"Lewis?"

Lou stops, fighting the urge to keep going. The door's two feet in front of him. Escape.

"What is it, Sheldon?"

The man begins to speak but stops. He finally points to all the papers on his desk.

"Do you know why I came to the office on a Saturday?"

"No, Sheldon, please tell me."

"I'm getting a jump on next week's payroll."

Lou just shrugs.

"I've advised your father several times to pay his employees once every two weeks, instead of every week. But he insists, even though it's more work for the firm. Do you know why?"

Lou just shrugs again. He feels for the letter opener

in his back pocket. It's heavy and sharp. It's practically a knife.

"Because, Lewis, your dad wants his employees to always have their money in hand. To be able to pay their rent or buy things or go to the movies. 'I don't want them to have to worry about anything, Sheldon.' That's what he always tells me. 'I just want them to be happy.'"

When Lou doesn't say anything, Sheldon adds, "He's a good man, Lewis."

Lou shakes his head and turns to go, but the office manager isn't done. He stands up quickly, causing half a dozen pieces of paper to fly off his desk and float to the floor.

"Lewis, give your dad a chance." His voice trembles, the opposite of the stiff and formal way he usually speaks. "He loves you."

"Yeah, well, he's got some funny ways of showing it."

"So do you."

•

Lou pulls Donato's letter opener and the latest request from the law firm from his back pocket as he gets into his dad's Mercedes. After placing them on the dashboard, he reaches for the leather gym bag in the back seat from where it sits on top of two wooden tennis rackets. He unzips the gym bag and places the opener and the letter on top of his tennis whites, which glow against the black inside the bag. He zips up the gym bag, tosses it to the floor in front of the passenger seat, and starts the car. The beach club is about twenty minutes away.

His parents joined the club as soon as they could afford it. It wasn't enough to just move to the suburbs, you also had to fit in. Once they heard about the club, and learned how many of their neighbors were members, his parents were determined to also join. But it took a few years. The rent in Brooklyn had been cheap and things were close; you didn't even need a car. In Long Island they had a mortgage, and everything was so spread out. When they first moved to Freeport, Sidney Reed was a treasurer at a plastics company called Cellu-Craft. It took time for him to work his way up the ladder, not to mention eventually go out on his own. They could only afford one car, which Lou's father took to the office every day. This left Lou's mother to go to the store on foot, his sister trailing behind because she was too young to attend school. Once Sidney Reed began to be successful, the family joined the beach club. Lou didn't fight it. More than a few of his friends' families were also members. He learned how to play tennis, got a tan, hung out on the beach, and ran up bills on his parents' account.

Pulling into the long driveway, Lou barely slows down as he approaches the guard booth. The guard sees the car, knows who it belongs to, and waves to Lou as he passes.

The main clubhouse sits at the end of a winding road lined with tall trees. Peeking through the trunks is a golf course with grass that looks unnaturally green. Even though it was built in the '40s, the building's designed to look like it's from the nineteenth century. It features red brick, tall columns, and an elaborate portico. Lou stops under the awning, shuts off the engine, and grabs the gym bag and tennis rackets. A young kid wearing a polo shirt with the club's crest on the pocket comes running over from a podium. He trades Lou the keys for a receipt for the car.

"Staying long, sir?"

The kitchen staff doesn't speak English, but the guys parking the cars are all local boys. This kid probably has some of the same teachers at Freeport High that Lou had.

"For dinner," Lou says, heading for the locker room.

The boy gives a salute and then hops into the Mercedes.

Lou changes into his tennis whites. The locker room's filled with men of all ages changing in and out of swimsuits, tennis gear, golfing clothes. The club is popular, and even on days when the weather's gorgeous and it seems like everyone in New York is at Jones Beach, the club is still full.

Lou heads out to the beach chairs, carrying the rackets. He sits down and orders a turkey sandwich from a dark-skinned attendant also wearing white. Lou had wanted to order a double scotch—he's still on edge from the week—but resisted, wanting to stay sharp for later. He hates to lose at tennis.

When his lunch arrives, Lou eats as he watches the waves break on the sand. On the beach, kids are making sandcastles and burying their parents. Kites are flying, Frisbees are tossed back and forth and, at the edge of the club's property, there's a high-spirited game of volleyball. When the waiter returns to retrieve the empty plate, Lou orders a piña colada. Twenty minutes later, he's mostly finished with the drink when he feels someone beside him.

"I thought I might find you here."

He looks up and sees his sister. They don't look a great

deal alike, but when they're together, you can tell they're brother and sister. They have the same dark and curly hair.

"Bunny!" He stands up and gives her a big hug. After the embrace, he looks her over. She's wearing jeans and a loose blouse patterned in peace signs. "Aren't we playing tennis?"

She slaps him playfully.

"Of course, Lou. I dropped off my stuff in the locker room. I wanted to come find you first to say hi."

As Lou grins, his sister reaches out to touch where the bruise has formed under his eye.

"Oh, sweetie, your face."

"It's nothing." He pushes her hand away. "You go change and I'll grab a court."

She looks skeptical but leans in for another hug before retreating to the locker room. She knows better than to question her brother about something he obviously wants to keep quiet. After she leaves, Lou leans down and grabs his drink. It's mostly just melted ice that tastes slightly of coconut, but he drinks it anyway.

The only court free is the one in the corner. It backs up onto the ocean and stands alongside rows and rows of beach chairs. When he was first learning the sport, Lou lobbed at least half a dozen balls right into the water. A few even landed amid the guests getting suntans. Whenever this happened, Lou always demanded they throw the ball back.

His sister emerges after a few minutes and, after a short warm-up, they begin a game. She plays well, making Lou run all over the court. And yet, despite his years of smoking—which slows him down considerably—he has an edge that his sister does not. Lou has a killer instinct.

She's just having a good time, but he wants to win. Out of four games, he wins three.

Afterward, they sit on the bench by the side of the court. The other courts are now empty, and most of the beach chairs are unoccupied. Everyone's changing for dinner. The sun's beginning to descend and the sky is turning pink on its way to purple. A cool breeze off the ocean dries the sweat on their skin, almost making them cold.

"You know," Lou says, staring out at the water, "if I could bring Seymour here, I'd have my two favorite things in the world. Dogs and the beach."

"What about music?" his sister says. "Where does that fit in?"

He wipes down his forehead with a towel.

"These days? Nowhere."

"You writing anything new?"

Lou laughs.

"With Mom and Dad and Grandma in the house? Besides, I think I've had enough of all that."

He almost tells her about his meeting the day before with Danny Fields, but decides against it. It's too depressing. All of that work, for nothing.

"You're *good*, Lou. The Velvet Underground was good. Whatever you do next will be good too."

He sits up.

"I've written some poems. Sent them to magazines. The *Harvard Advocate* just accepted one."

"Yeah, but Lou, won't you miss rock and roll?"

He laughs. "A better question is will rock and roll miss *me*?"

She shakes her head, not accepting this.

"When I saw you in Cleveland, in college, you guys were amazing. You can't turn your back on all that."

He just waves this away.

"You don't tell people I'm your brother, do you?"

"What do you mean?"

"Like in school, your medical classes." Lou takes the towel from around his neck and lets it fall to the ground. Behind them, they can hear noises coming from the dining room. Glasses clinking, chairs scraping against the floor, the low hum of conversation. "Never tell people you're related to me, I want you to promise."

His sister is shocked but also sad.

"Lou, but—I'm proud of you. I *like* telling people I'm your sister."

"Bunny," he says, grinning, "it's for your own good. Believe me."

"Okay, Lou. Whatever you say."

They enjoy the sunset for a few more minutes before Lou stands up.

"Let's go change," he says. "Mom and Dad are expecting us."

●

The family's seated in a corner of the main dining room, overlooking the green for the seventeenth hole. Sidney Reed has already made the rounds, shaking hands and saying hello to neighbors and clients. Lou's mom has gossiped a little with those seated nearby, and even Lou's sister has chatted with a friend who's also home from school. And while Lou had resisted ordering a scotch earlier in the day, nothing holds him back now. He'd downed his second Johnnie Walker Red before the salads even arrived.

"So, Lewis," his dad says after they've all been served soup, "I understand you were at the office today."

Lou looks up from his third drink.

"How did you know that?"

Sidney Reed blows on his bowl before dipping in his soup spoon.

"Sheldon called me."

"What, did he think I was robbing the place or something?"

Lou's sister and mom quietly eat their soup, not wanting to be drawn into what might turn into a fight.

"Not at all, Lewis. He had a question about payroll and wanted to get an answer before Monday." His father puts down his soup spoon and takes a sip of water. "Sheldon's a good worker. Goes in almost every weekend."

Lou pushes away the soup. His appetite has suddenly disappeared.

"You saying I'm *not* a good worker?"

"Now, boys," his mother says in a calming tone, "don't you start."

Lou touches her hand reassuringly.

"It's okay, Ma. I'm not starting anything." He turns to his dad. "I stopped by the public library yesterday. Read some books about copyright and got some forms. I was filling them out, that's all."

"Ah, yes," his dad says grandly. Resting his elbows on the table, Sidney Reed interlaces his fingers and rests his chin on his fists. "Your continuing trips to the city. How many does that make for this week? Two? Three?"

"I'll make it up to you next week, okay?" Lou drains the last of the scotch and tries to find a waiter to order another. "All of your letters are going to go out, don't worry."

"What I worry about, Lewis, is the effect your attitude may be having on the other workers. They're a fine bunch, and I don't want them to develop bad habits based on your example."

Unable to take any more, Lou reaches into his gym bag that sits under the table. He pulls out Donato's letter opener and slams it down on the table. It hits his soup spoon and makes a metallic clank. His family jumps and everyone in the dining room glances in their direction.

His mom looks first at the table, and then at her son.

"Lewis, what is that?"

Lou just stares at his father. Sidney Reed just stares back.

His sister asks, "Lou, what are you doing? What's happening?"

"Pops," Lou says, "you want to tell them, or should I?"

Sidney Reed still doesn't speak, but his pale face begins to turn red. Lou now pulls out the letter from the law firm about Donato's things. He throws this on the table too, only it lands silently.

"Tell them, Dad," Lou persists. "Tell them about the dead man."

"That's quite enough, Lewis."

His dad's voice is stern but even. People are watching. He doesn't want there to be a scene.

"Sid, I don't understand."

When Sidney Reed turns to his wife, his face softens.

"It's nothing, Toby, just business."

Lou snorts.

"Why don't you tell her what kind of business you're *really* in, Pops?"

This seems to make Sidney Reed snap. He rises quickly and, with one hand, gathers up the letter opener and the crumpled letter. With the other hand he pulls Lou by the arm and marches him through the dining room as if he were a child.

He leads Lou toward a small sitting area between the bathrooms and the kitchen. Men in white uniforms pass by carrying silver trays filled with food, drinks, dirty dishes.

"Lewis, I've had just about enough of your shenanigans this week. You need to control yourself."

"Why did you do it, Dad?"

"I don't know what you're talking about."

Sidney Reed puts the letter opener and the crumpled correspondence into the breast pocket of his blazer.

"Donato, Dad. The Sailor. I know all about it. I saw the file, I read the newspaper article. I even went to the storage place. Why, Dad? Why do you have his stuff? And why won't you give it back?"

"It's complicated, Lewis. And we shouldn't talk about it here, of all places."

"Yes, Pops, we're going to talk about it. And here. I want to know what's happening."

Sidney Reed lets out a huge breath before speaking.

"I did it for you, Lewis."

"Me? What does it have to do with me?"

"I read in the newspaper about the man's death. And I knew that you'd known him. I knew that you'd been to his apartment."

"How?"

"We saw you shortly after it happened. You came by on your way to Boston. You bragged about what a sordid scene you'd witnessed."

"I told you about the shooting?"

Sidney Reed considers this.

"Not in so many words, but you told me enough." He speaks softly, not wanting anyone passing by to hear. "You were always trying to shock us. Shoving disgusting details in our faces and hoping to get a reaction. I connected what you'd said to what I'd read in the paper."

While Lou doesn't remember this, he recognizes it as his general behavior. It isn't enough that he'd escaped Freeport. He had to make sure everyone around him registered his disdain.

"Okay, but what happened then? How did you get his things?"

Sidney Reed smiles slightly, as if—years later—he's still impressed with himself and what he'd done.

"I went to his building and talked to the super. I pretended that the veteran was a client and that we had to store his belongings for tax purposes. The super didn't know any better. There hadn't been any relatives, and the police were barely investigating. The super just wanted the stuff gone so he could rent out the apartment to someone else. He probably knew I was lying and didn't care."

"So, you put his stuff in storage? Why?"

Sidney Reed steps closer to his son. When he speaks again, it's a whisper.

"I wanted to protect you, Son."

"From what?"

Sidney Reed shakes his head before continuing.

"Things were starting to happen for you, Lewis. That record you'd made with that painter was about to come out. Your band seemed to be a success. You were in the papers. Everything you'd always wanted, going all the way back to when you were in high school, was starting to come true. I just—I wanted you to do well."

"But how did the Sailor affect me? Just because I was there?"

Sidney Reed hesitates, as if he doesn't want to say what he's about to say.

"You brought something with you when you came to see us. After that party, before you went to Boston. You said you wanted to drop off something, keep it at our house for a while. That's why you'd stopped by. I thought you meant a guitar or clothes or something. But that's not what it was."

Lou tries to remember the visit, but can't.

"What was it, Pops? What did I leave at the house?"

"A gun."

A dishwasher carrying a steel tray full of mugs—steam coming off them—crashes through the double doors that leads from the kitchen. Besides the workers passing through, the sitting room is empty. They both sit down.

"You were tense, jumpy," he continues. "Like when we had to go get you at NYU. I thought maybe you were getting sick again. That's why I did what I did."

"What did you do, Dad?"

"I was worried about you, Lewis."

"Dad, what did you *do*?"

Sidney Reed hangs his head.

"I went through your things. That's when I found it. It was in your closet. A black revolver. Loaded."

"And you thought I killed him?"

Sidney Reed reaches down and takes Lou's hands in his. The old man's palms are as smooth as polished stones.

"No, Son. Not for a second. But I didn't want to take any chances. I told you, I wanted to protect you. Your whole life would have been over if—"

"If what, Pops?"

"If the police saw the man's things—especially that painting—and started putting it all together. You could have been a suspect. You could have"—he pauses for a second, not even wanting to say it—"you could have gone to jail. Your whole life would have been over. I couldn't let that happen to you."

Lou remembers something from the storage facility.

"Donato's things, Dad. It's just his furniture. All his personal stuff is gone. No clothes. No papers. Where did all of it go?"

Sidney Reed pauses again before speaking. A jet can be heard flying overhead.

"After everything was transferred to Twenty-Third Street, Sheldon and I went down there on a weekend. We went through all of the veteran's possessions and removed anything that we thought might be . . . incriminating."

"Like, his clothes?"

"I didn't want to take any chances, Son. We didn't have time to go through pockets or things like that, so we just put whatever looked like it could be traced back to the man into filing boxes and got rid of them."

"What did you do with it all?"

"I don't know. Shelly disposed of it. He never told me where, and I never asked."

"Sheldon Mayer did that?"

"He's a good friend, Lewis. And he cares about the firm."

Lou points to his dad's jacket.

"But what about the letter opener? He must have kept that. Maybe he kept other things too."

Sidney Reed looks ashamed.

"No, Son. That was me. I'd found it in his desk and was using it to open his mail. I wanted to see if you'd sent him any letters. I was looking for anything that might connect you to him. But there were too many and Shelly convinced me to just throw out everything in case we missed something. I must have put the letter opener in my pocket and forgotten about it. And then maybe your mother discovered it when she was doing the laundry. But I don't know how it ended up at the office. Until tonight, I hadn't seen it since that day in Manhattan with Shelly."

The mention of his mother makes Lou ask a question.

"Does Mom know about any of this?"

"No, Lewis, and I don't want her to know. She would just worry." Sidney Reed produces a handkerchief from his pocket and pats his forehead. "She adores you, Son. If she thought you were in any kind of trouble, it would just kill her. Do you understand? The last couple of years have been hard enough."

"'Last couple of years,' what do you mean?"

Sidney Reed sighs again.

"The traveling, that crowd you were running around with. We never knew where you were, and you hardly called. There were all those articles in the paper about that painter." Sidney Reed never approved of Warhol, barely even speaks his name. "We're your parents, Lewis. We wanted to make sure you were okay. That you were happy."

They sit in silence for a few moments, waiters continuing to walk back and forth in the hallway with full or empty trays. Saturday night at the club is always busy.

"But Dad, that law firm." Lou points at his father's chest. "The letters. Donato has a relative and they want his stuff. They're *entitled* to his stuff."

"I was hoping—I thought we could just stall." Sidney Reed wipes down his forehead again with the handkerchief. "Buy some more time. I thought maybe it would all somehow just go away."

"But, Dad, you've been hanging on to this stuff for years. And now someone's come looking for it. We need to just—you need to give it all back."

Sidney Reed nods, as if finally deciding something.

"Okay, Son. You're right. It's time to end this." After giving his face one more wipe with the handkerchief, he puts it back into his pocket. "On Monday you can write to that law firm and tell them we're prepared to return the veteran's possessions. Tell them we were wrong about the audit, it was all just a big mistake. We'll release the man's things as soon as they like. We'll even pay to have them moved."

Now Lou nods.

They're returning to the dining room when Lou grabs his dad's arm and stops him.

"Pops, the carpet."

"What carpet?"

"There's a carpet. A rug with a bloodstain. It was rolled up, but I knocked it over. It's with all of Donato's stuff."

"And you think it contains the man's blood?"

Lou nods, adding, "I think I wrote about it in a song. On one of my records."

Sidney Reed thinks about this. Lou takes the opportunity to look through the dining room. He can see his mom and sister searching for them. Lou tries to wave reassuringly.

His dad finally says, "I have to go back."

"And do what?"

"Get the carpet, Son. And get rid of it."

"Are you sure?"

His father's eyes twinkle.

"I got rid of his things before. I can do it again."

Thinking of the punches he'd taken yesterday, Lou says, "Okay, but I'm not going to let you go alone."

SUNDAY

L OU WAKES UP with a hangover. After he and his dad returned to their table the night before, Lou resumed downing drink after drink. His father finally began waving off the waiters before Lou could order another. By the end of the evening, Lou was slurring his speech and stumbling around the dining room. He had to be helped back to the Mercedes. His father drove him home while his mom dropped off his sister at a friend's in the Lincoln.

Lou sits up slowly. His stomach feels okay, but his head is throbbing. After sitting still for a few minutes and drinking a glass of water that sits on his bedside table, the throbbing goes away. Even the bruise on his face, and his split lip from Friday, are beginning to feel a bit better.

He swings out his legs, planting them firmly on the floor. When Lou is sure the room has stopped spinning, he opens his eyes. The closet door is open, and he sees again his yearbook and diploma leaning against the shoebox. The shoebox is from high school. It had previously housed a pair of size 8 penny loafers he'd long ago misplaced. When he reaches for the shoebox, he discovers it's heavier than it should be. He'd used it in high school to store small mementos and keepsakes. Letters and a few cards couldn't weigh this much.

He places the shoebox beside him on the bed. Taking off the lid, he sees a greeting card. The front shows the photo of a lone figure walking along the beach at either dusk or dawn, footprints in the sand being erased by waves. Lou opens the card. Inside is printed, in italic script, *Love on your birthday and always*. Below this, surrounded by a field of white, his mother's handwriting. *Mom & Dad.*

Reaching past the half-dozen other cards and letters, Lou sees what gives the box its weight. A black revolver— the gun his dad mentioned the night before. He picks it up. The metal actually looks blue and not black. The curved wooden handle is carved with small diamonds, and the trigger and hammer are brushed steel, gray. The nose is short, barely two inches long. It's nothing like the silver pistols he'd played with as a boy, the ones that hold a roll of caps and are as long and shiny as a flute. Bringing the revolver to his nose, all he can smell is oil.

He's seen enough westerns to know you can tell by looking at the barrel whether a gun is loaded or not. Pointing the stubby nose toward the floor, he sees that most of the holes are filled. The end of each bullet is dulled brass with a small silver center. Lou begins to turn the barrel with his thumb. It makes a clicking noise as it rotates. Lou counts only one empty hole. A single shot has been fired.

Lou's transferring the gun from his right hand to his left when someone knocks on his door. The noise startles him, causing him to drop the revolver.

"Lewis, you joining us for breakfast?"

"Yeah, Ma," he calls out, his voice hoarse. "Be there in a minute."

She retreats, footsteps echoing down the hallway.

Lou nervously looks down. The gun landed on top of a notebook that is open on the floor to a new song he'd started to write the other day. The revolver blocks out most of the lyrics but, at the top, he can see the word VICIOUS written in capital letters. He covers up the gun with a corner of the comforter and heads out to breakfast.

In the living room, his grandmother is watching TV and eating a bagel while his mom is walking around doing various chores. Putting away dishes, tidying couch cushions, picking up sections of newspaper that sit at the foot of his dad's recliner. Lou shuffles to the kitchen. The counter is filled with a brown bag of assorted bagels along with containers of lox, whitefish, and cream cheese. For now, all he wants is coffee.

He sits down at the dining room table with a heavy mug. He can hear the TV from the living room. *A thunder of jets in an open sky, a streak of gray, and a cheerful "Hi!"* After drinking half a cup—which seems to actually make his headache worse—he gets up and pulls an everything bagel from the brown bag. As he's slicing the bagel in half, he notices his hands are shaking. He puts down the knife and places both hands on the Formica counter, steadying himself. He closes his eyes and breathes in and out slowly.

"Feeling okay, dear?"

He opens his eyes. His mom is standing next to him, a worried look on her face.

"Yeah, Ma," Lou answers. "It's nothing. Just a little tired, that's all."

She's used to seeing him like this in the morning. Even in high school, Lou came to breakfast with ferocious hangovers. Both parents knew better than to ask what he'd done the night before, if only because they knew he would tell them.

She pats his left arm and returns to her chores. Lou spreads cream cheese on the bagel and returns to the table. He's still eating when his dad comes in from the garage. Sidney Reed is wearing old slacks and a flannel shirt. It's about as casual as he gets. Making sure his wife isn't listening, he sidles up to Lou.

"We're all set, Son," he says quietly. "When do you want to go?"

It takes Lou a few seconds to remember the plan from the night before. The storage facility. The stained rug. Tomorrow, Lou will write to the law firm saying they can have Donato's things. That should be the end of it.

"Give me five minutes, okay, Pops? I want to finish my bagel."

His mom spots them speaking in hushed tones.

"What are you boys up to?"

"Nothing, Ma," Lou replies. He tries to smile, but his hangover makes it difficult.

"Actually, Toby," Sidney Reed says, "Lewis and I have to run a few errands this afternoon. In the city. We'll be gone most of the day."

"Okay," she says, skeptically, "but if you're going to miss dinner, make sure you call."

"Of course, sweetheart."

Sidney Reed winks at Lou and then goes back to the

garage. Lou finishes his bagel and coffee, puts his dishes in the sink, and returns to his room. He trades his pajamas for jeans and a T-shirt, also pulling on a Syracuse sweater. As he ties his shoes, he sees the corner of his notebook. Pulling back the comforter reveals the gun. As he slips the notebook out from underneath the revolver, he sees some of the lyrics he wrote earlier in the week.

You stepped on her hands and you held her feet
You're not the kind of person that I want to meet

He closes the notebook and places it on his nightstand. Lou doesn't want to leave the gun on the floor, but he also doesn't want to use the shoebox again. It's too small for the other things he also wants to hide. He puts the gun on his bed and searches his room for something big enough to hold the pistol, Donato's address book, and the film can.

At the back of his closet he finds a small brown suitcase. It's old and worn, the leather scuffed at the corners. He used it for trips when he was in high school, staying overnight with relatives in Brooklyn. He also used it in college when he came home on the weekends or for holidays. Lou opens the suitcase and places it on the bed. He wraps the gun in a T-shirt and places it inside. Looking across the room he sees the metal film can sitting near his stereo. His parents' copy of *White Light/White Heat* is still on the turntable. Lou reaches for the film can, but then pauses. He remembers something. He turns to his dresser. In the top drawer, under a pile of tube socks with red-and-blue stripes, he sees what he's looking for. The silver locket. He grabs it and quickly shoves it into his pocket.

"Lewis," his dad calls from the living room, "let's go!"

"One second, Pops."

Lou finds Donato's address book sitting on his desk directly beneath a felt pennant on the wall that says GO DEVILS. He picks up the book and quickly flips through it, looking for the address he'd seen the other day. The one that's been crossed out. He finds it, rips out the page, and adds it to the pocket that holds the locket. Then he tosses the address book and the film can into the suitcase. He zips it up and places it back into the closet.

Lou emerges from his room. His dad is pacing around the kitchen, and his mom has finally sat down in the dining room to have a bagel of her own.

"Bye, Mom."

When Lou leans in to give her a kiss on the cheek, he can smell her perfume. It reminds him of being a boy in Brooklyn and being tucked into bed, that final kiss of the night.

"Now, you boys be careful," she says.

"We will," he replies. "We will."

•

Once they're on the turnpike, Lou's the first to speak.

"I found the gun this morning, Dad."

Sidney Reed doesn't say anything; he just keeps his eyes on the road.

"I may have done it," Lou continues. "You have to realize that. Keep that possibility open."

"Lewis, you're not a killer."

"How do you know?"

"A father knows what his children are capable of, for things good and bad." He switches lanes, despite the solid white line. "And despite any flaws you may have, you couldn't have done that. I'm positive."

Lou sits forward and places his head in his hands. He rubs his temples with his palms, trying to make memories rise to the surface.

"I just wish I could remember."

"You don't recall anything from that night?"

"No, nothing. My memory's been shot ever since . . ."

"The hospital," Sidney Reed answers. "I know."

Lou looks over at him.

"Why did you do it, Dad? Why did you take me there?"

"The psychiatrists—they told us it would *help* you. We just wanted you to be better, you have to know that."

"Yeah, but shock treatment? How was that going to help?"

"Son, when you came home from college that first time you weren't yourself. You were anxious. You barely spoke. All the light had gone from your eyes. We just wanted to get it back, for your sake. Your life was just beginning."

Traffic slows the Mercedes to almost a standstill. Sidney Reed turns to look at his son. Tears fill the man's eyes.

"Lewis, there's not a day that goes by I don't regret what we did to you. What I *let* happen. For that I am sorry, but you can't blame me forever."

"I don't know about 'forever,' but I can sure as hell blame you now."

Sidney Reed slouches in his seat as he turns back to the road. The traffic has thinned out and cars start moving again.

"You have no idea what it's like to be a parent, Lewis."

"What, Pops. What's it like?"

"You and your sister are the most important things to me in the world. And maybe I don't say it very well when we're together, but let me tell you how extremely proud I am of you and how much I love and cherish you. I didn't mean to hurt you."

Lou doesn't say anything. They both just stare forward as the city begins to slowly come into view. You can see the tips of skyscrapers and dozens of water towers. Buildings, windows, billboards. It's hard to believe there's a river between here and there, that what you're looking at is an island.

Lou and his father are silent as they enter the midtown tunnel on their way to the storage facility. Emerging into the bright sunlight of Manhattan, Lou speaks again, telling his dad to go past the building. They park the Mercedes around the corner, on Tenth Avenue.

Walking into the office, Lou's glad to see that the old man from earlier in the week isn't there. Instead, sitting behind the desk, is a young black guy with a large Afro. Knowing the routine, Lou signs in on the clipboard and requests the key for space 919. After he writes down the time, Lou flips through the pages to see if anyone else has paid a visit to the space since Friday.

"Is there a problem?" asks the man as he gets up from the desk.

"Nope," says Lou, pushing the clipboard across the

counter. He takes the key and he and his father ride the elevator to the ninth floor.

As they walk down the hallway, Lou asks, "When was the last time you were here?"

"I was only here that one time, with Sheldon. Before that, movers handled everything. All I did was pay the bills."

Lou inserts the key and fights with the door to get it open. The Warhol, sitting on the chair, greets them. Lou just pushes it aside.

"There, Pops." He points. "The carpet."

Sidney Reed nods.

"Okay, let's get it and go."

Lou steps sideways into the space. Nudging the throne chair with his legs, the one he'd seen in Donato's movie, he grabs one end of the white rug. It had come unfurled when it fell the other day, so Lou has to lay it on the floor in the hallway to roll it back up. When his dad sees the dark-purple stain, he looks away.

"Okay, Pops, help me get this to the elevator."

Downstairs, Lou quickly returns the key and signs out. As he and his dad carry the rolled-up rug to the car, Lou looks back at the tall, orange-brick building. He hopes this is the last time he ever has to come here, will ever have to see Donato's things.

The rug barely fits in the trunk of the Mercedes. They have to wedge it in diagonally, and even then it fights with the spare and a tire jack for space. It would have easily fit in the back seat, but neither Lou nor his father wanted it in the car with them.

After slamming the trunk shut, Sidney Reed looks at his son.

"Now what?"

Their plan last night had only taken them this far. They hadn't decided what to do with the rug, beyond just wanting to get rid of it.

"I know what to do," Lou finally says. "Get in. I'll drive."

●

The piers are just a few blocks away, but Lou has trouble finding the best approach. He'd only ever walked there from the subway or taken a cab.

A hundred years ago, when New York City was a major port, the edge of almost all of Lower Manhattan held a dock or a pier in order to receive ships large and small. It was an island and, before bridges were built and the automobiles to ride on them, everything came in by water. All the piers on the west side are now run-down and dirty. They sit, dilapidated, in the shadow of the elevated highway that runs alongside them. The long buildings where goods had been collected after being hauled off the huge ships are in disrepair. Wooden pilings have been left to rot in the dirty water of the Hudson. During the day, people come here to sunbathe or cruise, and at night it's often a den of anonymous gay sex. If you're uptown, you go to the Ramble. If you're downtown, you go to the piers.

Lou parks the Mercedes as close to the dock as he can. They get out, pull the rug from the trunk, and begin to walk toward the water's edge. And while it certainly looks suspicious, no one stops them. No one even looks at them.

Sidney Reed glances around as they approach the water.

"How do you know this area, Lewis?"

Lou grins and says, "You don't want to know."

They have to step over a rotting wood railing to get close enough to the river's edge so that the rug will land in the water and not on the rocks directly beneath them.

Lou asks, "Ready?"

His dad nods and, after swinging it back and forth three times to get momentum, they heave the stained carpet into the river.

It doesn't make a splash. It barely even makes any ripples. In a second, it's gone. Just another piece of trash thrown into the Hudson.

They turn and start walking back to the car.

"You know," Sidney Reed sighs, "I feel like a weight's been lifted off my chest."

"Why?"

"I've been worried about this whole thing for years." He motions back to the water. "The idea that it's all going to be over soon is a great relief."

Lou looks at his dad. He can see himself in the man's profile. That chin and nose, those eyes he's known for as long as he can remember. It's all part of him no matter how hard he tries to reject it.

"Why didn't you ever come to me with this, Pops?"

"It was my responsibility, Lewis. I took it on. It was my idea, and so it was my burden to keep."

Lou kicks at an empty can of Schlitz.

"You know, Dad, you're involved in this now too. Accessory after the fact."

"Well then"—Sidney Reed reaches out and touches his son's shoulder—"we'll just have to make sure we don't get caught."

As they walk farther and farther away from the docks, the sound of the water lapping against the decaying pilings grows fainter while the sound of traffic gets louder. When the Mercedes is about ten feet away, Lou says, "Pops, I want to make one more stop."

The smile disappears, worry once again clouding his father's face.

"Son, we've been gone long enough. Your mother—"

"Please, Dad."

Sidney Reed closes his eyes and nods.

"Okay, Lewis."

They get into the car, Sidney Reed behind the wheel this time.

"Where are we going?"

Lou digs the page from Donato's address book out of his pocket.

"Connecticut."

•

The house isn't easy to find. They have to stop at two gas stations and ask directions. Even then they get lost, having to turn around in a cul-de-sac more than once as they navigate the twisty, tree-lined streets of Fairfield.

The neighborhoods look similar to the ones in Freeport except the homes are older and bigger, the streets narrower and more curved. And whereas their own house is only twenty years old, the homes in Connecticut seem to date back to the beginning of the century. Sometimes it shows, with peeling paint, drooping eaves, and chimneys that lean.

The address they're looking for is toward the end of the block, directly across from a vacant lot and next to a park full of rusting structures. Sidney Reed pulls up behind some metal trash cans and parks the Mercedes next to the curb.

"Stay in the car, Pops."

"Son, please," Sidney Reed protests, even though he's not sure what he's protesting, "you don't have to do this alone."

Lou's too tired to fight back. They both get out of the car.

It's a big house, three stories, but it needs a coat of paint and a few repairs. As they walk on the winding cement pathway that leads to the front door, Lou looks at the park next to the house. He sees a slide, three crooked swings, and a merry-go-round that sits at a tilt. He'd written and recorded a song called "Merry Go Round" after getting out of high school. Back then, he felt held back by everything. His age, his parents, Long Island. All he wanted to do was escape to the city, start his life, have some excitement. He figures the girl who'd once lived in this house felt the same way.

Stepping onto the porch, it creaks. Lou knocks, lightly, twice.

The door's answered by a boy, probably about fourteen. He has a bad teenage mustache and long blond hair, and the bottom of his belly peeks out under the hem of an Emerson, Lake & Palmer T-shirt.

"Hi," Lou says, a bit uncertainly. "I'm—is your dad home?"

"No," the boy replies. "My dad doesn't live here anymore. But my mom is."

"Can we see her?" When the boy doesn't move or seem to react, Lou adds, "It's about Kathy."

The boy looks them up and down before retreating into the house and shouting for his mother. She comes to the door a minute later, the boy looking over her shoulder. She's wearing a burgundy house coat and her graying hair is pulled back. Lou recognizes her as one of the two faces in the silver locket.

"Come in," she says, her voice soft.

All four of them walk to a living room that overlooks the street. Lou and his dad sit on the couch. She sits in a chair while the boy continues to hover. Noticing his presence, she says, calmly, "Jason, go play outside."

"Aw, Mom, do I have to?"

"Yes, Jason, go."

The boy slinks out of the room. The front door opens and closes.

"Are you detectives?"

Sidney Reed leans forward and says, with respect, "No, ma'am, we're accountants."

She looks confused.

"How did you know Kathy?"

Lou clears his voice before speaking.

"I never knew your daughter, but I think I have something that belongs to her."

He reaches into his pocket, pulls out the necklace, and

hands it to the woman. After opening it, she breaks down in tears.

Wiping her eyes, she says, "After they found her body, they gave me her things. I didn't want the dress, or those silly shoes. I just wanted the locket. We gave it to her for her Sweet Sixteen. She disappeared almost exactly a year later." She looks up. "Where did you get this?"

Lou answers, "In the things of a man who's now dead."

"The police," she says. "Have you told the police?"

"Not yet, ma'am," Lou says. "But I will."

Sidney Reed pulls a business card from his wallet and gives it to the woman. He says, "We will do everything we can. I promise."

She places the card in a small candy dish that sits under an imitation Tiffany lamp. She continues to clutch the locket.

"I told her not to go to New York. I begged her. We both did."

"Ma'am?" says Sidney Reed, as if asking permission to speak. "I know the pain of losing a child. Not in the way that you have, of course. But I've felt what it's like to have a child you've raised and loved go so far away, you don't think they'll ever come back."

Lou turns uneasily in his seat.

"Our children make their own decisions," he continues, "and we have to accept that, even if it takes them far away from us. You did everything you could. You provided a home, you raised her. What happens after that is out of our hands. You can't blame yourself for what happened."

They can hear the boy in the park next door on the merry-go-round as it creaks while making wobbly circles.

Still staring at the locket, she says, "Her brother's all I have left. I don't want to make the same mistake."

"All you can do is give love," Sidney Reed says. "And offer patience and acceptance. If you do that, all will be well."

The woman says, in a whisper, "Thank you."

Lou and his dad get up from the sofa. She walks them to the door.

Seeing that they're leaving, the boy jumps off the merry-go-round and runs back to the house. He passes Lou and his father as they step down from the porch.

The door slams shut as Lou and his dad reach the Mercedes. Turning to look back at the house, they can see into the living room. They watch as the woman envelops her son in an embrace so tight it seems she might never let him go.

Lou and his dad get into the Mercedes.

Sniffling slightly, Sidney Reed says, "Come on, Son, we'd better get home. You know how your mother is."

MONDAY

"Lou, you goin' on a trip?"

He looks up and sees Vera heading toward him, pushing the silver cart loaded with mail and files. She's wearing the same gold-and-black jacket with velvet trim she wore last week.

"What?"

She points to the brown suitcase that stands next to his desk, the one he'd packed the day before. It holds the gun, can of film, and Donato's address book. Lou didn't like the idea of leaving it at the house. Lou figures at lunch he'll toss it into one of the dumpsters underneath the train station.

"Nah, Vera," he says, grinning. "That's my briefcase. I'm a businessman now."

She laughs, adds a pile of mail to the other stacks surrounding his typewriter, and moves on to the next desk.

The day is just starting. Ray's handing out the coffees, the secretaries are talking about the weekend, and Sheldon Mayer is in the corner looking annoyed. Someone brought in donuts. The pink bakery box is open on Audrey's desk, and the smell of maple and powdered sugar is in the air.

Lou turns back to his desk and opens Donato's file, which his father gave to him that morning. Lou quickly finds the letter he saw the previous Monday. Reading it again, the signature catches his eye. *Miss Rayon*. He had initially taken that to be a secretary, or an assistant, but now it seems oddly familiar. Lou also realizes the letter isn't on any sort of printed stationery or company letterhead. Instead, the address and name of the law firm—ROSIE, SALLY, AND DUCK—are merely typed. Last week, this had all looked official. Today it sets off alarms. Miss Rayon. Rosie, Sally, Duck. As Ray approaches with a Styrofoam cup, Lou figures it out. "Sister Ray." They're all characters in the song.

"Lou, you okay?" Ray places the cup of coffee onto one of the few spaces of the desk's surface not filled with mail.

Lou looks up.

"What? Oh, yeah, Ray. Never better."

Lou takes a quick swig of the coffee as Ray moves on to his last delivery, heading for Moira's desk.

Turning back to the letter, Lou looks at the address.

80-45 Winchester Boulevard
Building 74
Queens Village, NY 11427

The other day that had seemed legitimate too. Law firms could be anywhere, so why not in Queens? But now it causes a strange ring in his head.

"Winchester."

Saying the word, it feels familiar. As a kid playing cow-boys and Indians, he knew of a type of rifle called a Winchester, but that's not what it makes Lou think of now.

"Winchester. Winchester."

Every time he says it, something seems to shake loose. His memory is like a fog slowly lifting. But he still can't quite make a connection.

A bookcase along the back wall, sitting between two tall beige filing cabinets, holds stacks of phone books, yellow pages, and local maps. Lou gets up and searches the shelves until he finds what he's looking for. He places the huge, weathered book on an unoccupied desk. It's a street directory for all of New York City. He looks up Winchester in the index and flips through the large, waxy pages. When he finds it, he traces the street's path with his finger, looking for the address of the supposed law firm. The road crosses under both the Cross Island Parkway and the Grand Central Parkway. Finally, he finds it. It looks to be a cluster of small streets just down the road from Creedmoor Psychiatric Center, the place where he'd been taken as a teenager for shock treatments.

Lou gets up and walks across the room, stopping in the doorway of his father's office.

"Sheldon," Lou turns and calls out, "where's my dad?"

He looks up from a pair of huge ledgers. "Your father will be gone until at least lunch, Lewis. Had to drive all the way out to Montauk to see a client."

Lou walks back to his desk in a daze. He passes Moira, who is once again teaching Vera basic bookkeeping. She's saying, "That's good, Vera. That's *very* good."

Lou sits back down at his desk and picks up the letter. For the first time, he notices there isn't a phone number, nor is there any name other than "Miss Rayon." The fact that the address is on the same street as the hospital seems like more than just a coincidence. He closes his eyes, does his best to block out the hum of the office, and tries to remember.

It had been early summer that first time they took him to Creedmoor. Lou ended up having to go three times a week for two months. Twenty-four shocks in all.

He didn't know, when they first hauled him all the way out there, what was going to happen. He'd spoken to psychiatrists before. Answered all the standard questions. That first time, he just thought he was in for more of the same. When he saw the huge building—it's seventeen stories tall and you can see it from the turnpike—he knew he was in trouble. This was something new. Something bad.

The large parking lot was enclosed by a tall iron fence. Across the street was a park. There were always a few dozen kids there playing baseball or football. Kids not much younger than Lou. He always wished the Mercedes would take a left and not a right, enter the park and not the hospital, but it never did.

Even though the building itself looked industrial— you would have thought it was some sort of factory, or maybe a prison—the lobby almost looked normal. There was an information desk and bank of elevators. Gift shop and newsstand. If it weren't for the patients tied to gurneys, some of whom were screaming, or the unshaven men in bathrobes wandering around muttering gibberish, you might have thought it was any office in Manhattan.

Upstairs, the waiting rooms were filled with sobbing families and frightened patients. Going from office to office, and into the treatment rooms, felt like making your way through a giant maze. The whole place was nothing but corridors, and then there was the endless locking and unlocking of doors. In one room you waited. In another you changed into a thin dressing gown. The room where the shocks were given was small, with nothing inside but the big machine.

Lou had to first take a sedative. Then he was strapped to a gurney and wheeled into the room. A nurse would apply salve to his temple and stick a clamp in his mouth to make sure he didn't bite or swallow his tongue. Conductors with thick wires leading back to the machine were attached to his head.

Everyone got the same voltage, regardless of their size or symptoms. "Relax," the nurse would always tell him, "we're trying to help you." Overhead was a fluorescent light. Lou always focused on the light. He wondered why it didn't dim when they gave him the shock. Afterward, his body wouldn't stop twitching. He also couldn't remember anything. Not the car ride to Creedmoor, much less anything that had led to why he was there. His mom and dad had to help him down the hall, into the elevator, and back out to the car. No one ever spoke on the way home. What was there to talk about?

"Hey, Lou." Ray again approaches the desk. He's holding a glazed donut in each hand. "They're going fast. You want one?"

Lou, still holding the letter, shakes his head. As Ray walks away, Lou calls out to him.

"Raymond, you still got that GTO of yours?"

He turns around and grins.

"Fastest hot rod in all of New York. Parked just downstairs."

Lou stands up, folds the letter into quarters, and slides it into his back pocket.

"Wanna give me a lift?"

"You serious? Hell yeah."

Lou grabs the suitcase and starts to head toward the door. Ray follows. As they pass the desks, all the secretaries turn to watch.

●

They fly down the turnpike. Ray weaves in and out of traffic, changing lanes and whipping around any car that isn't moving as fast as he is. Whenever Lou's parents drove him to Creedmoor, it took a half hour. The way Ray's driving, it's only going to take ten minutes.

"Ray," Lou says loud enough to be heard over the roar of the engine, "I didn't say it was an emergency."

He just laughs and replies, "Aw, Lou, this is the way I always drive."

Lou had been holding the suitcase in his lap. Now he raises it to block his view out the windshield.

"What'd you bring that for, anyway?"

"Not sure," says Lou. "Figured it might come in handy."

As they get off the turnpike, Lou directs Ray to take a left and then a right. Ray finally slows down as they pass Creedmoor.

"What is that place?"

"It's a mental institution, Ray. You ever seen one?"

"Nah. Well, just the office."

The road rises and curves as they drive under a freeway. They pass a depot of garbage trucks and then a seminary. When the road transitions to houses, Lou says, "It must be the other direction."

Ray pulls into a driveway and turns around. When they cruise by Creedmoor a second time, Lou tries not to look.

Further down the road, Ray pulls into the driveway. There's a guard shack, but no one's inside, so they just keep driving. Three buildings surround the small parking lot. The one directly in front is made of red brick and has a white dormer on top, along with a weather vane. It looks like a post office in New Hampshire. The buildings flanking this are more plain, rectangles with windows. Looking to the left and right Lou sees streets and more buildings. Green, leafy trees are surrounded by patches of grass that need to be mowed.

Lou points and says, "Over there."

Ray pulls the GTO up to a large sign that says CREEDMOOR CAMPUS DIRECTORY. The map shows streets and numbered buildings. Lou pulls out the letter from last week and looks at the sign, muttering, "Building 74, Building 74." He finally finds it. The Helping Hands Transitional Residence is nestled between Mental Hygiene Legal Service and the Queens Developmental Disabilities Hillside Campus.

"Ray, go straight and then take a left."

The GTO idles down the quiet streets. They pass a chapel and a white gazebo that stands in a field of weeds. In the main wing of Creedmoor patients were found dead in their cells, beaten to death while bound in a straitjacket. The staff had blackjacks, Lou had seen them dangling from the belts of the orderlies. The whole building smelled like paraldehyde. But this looks like a village, or maybe a community college. Everything may be drab and run-down, but this is paradise compared to being locked up in the big building.

"Okay, Ray. Right over there."

The car rolls to a stop. There's a sign on the lawn, white words against a blue background. HELPING HANDS TRANSITIONAL RESIDENCE. BUILDING 74.

"Lou, I should—I got to get back to the office." Ray's fingers nervously knead the leather covering of his steering wheel. "I got, you know, stuff to do."

"No worries, Ray. I'll grab a cab back." Lou clutches the suitcase and gets out of the car. "Thanks for the ride."

As soon as Lou closes the door, Ray peels out. In a second the growl of the engine disappears and is replaced by silence. Lou takes a deep breath and enters the building.

The ground floor holds a kitchen and a large dining room. There are circular tables with tablecloths and linen napkins. Lou passes an activity room with a TV and long rows of tables holding puzzles and playing cards. A few older men sit watching a soap opera. Toward the back is a laundry room and, next to this, a staircase. Lou climbs the stairs.

Most of the doors along the second floor's long hallway are open. Lou sees the same things in each room. Twin bed and dresser. Radiator and desk. Personal possessions like photos or plants, a radio or stack of books. Small things to try to make it feel more like home.

Turning the corner and going down another hallway, he looks into a room and sees himself. He thinks it's a mirror, but then he notices his hair is shorter and he's wearing sunglasses and a black leather jacket. He's also standing next to Sterling Morrison. Moe's there too, along with Nico and John Cale. It's a photograph.

He enters the room slowly. It's the same as the others except for a lime-green rug and a record player sitting on a wooden milk crate turned on its side. A dozen albums sit on the floor, some leaning against the crate and some leaning against the off-white wall. On the dresser is a collection of amber pill bottles. Lou looks them over. Mellaril, Compazine, Trilafon, Stelazine, Prolixin. They're all prescribed to Timothy Steensma. The name doesn't mean anything to Lou.

Taped all around the room are clippings about the Velvet Underground. The band had never received much press, but every story that Lou can remember seems to be on the walls. There are also a few articles about Warhol, including his *Time* magazine cover and the front page of *Newsday* from when he was almost killed. ACTRESS SHOOTS ANDY WARHOL.

"Well, well, well, look who it is. The prodigal son."

Lou spins around, dropping the suitcase onto the green rug. A man stands in the doorway. He's slightly shorter than Lou and a few years older. He's wearing a wrinkled button-down shirt and brown polyester pants that are too long. The cuffs in the back are torn and ragged, and only the tips of black shoes poke out in the front.

"You don't remember me, do you?"

"Sorry," Lou says cautiously, "my memory's not what it used to be."

The man laughs darkly. "You and me both."

As the man enters the room and begins to admire the photos and news stories on the wall, Lou backs up.

"Are you"—Lou points to the rows of bottles—"Timothy Steensma?"

The man nods imperceptibly as he continues to gaze at all the clippings.

"The storage place," Lou finally says. "That was you."

Steensma turns to face him.

"It's nothing personal, Lou. I just want the painting."

Lou recognizes the voice.

"And that was you on Brigid's tape. From Max's."

The man turns back to the wall of articles and stories.

"*Loved* the second set. Shame you had to break up the band."

Lou looks around the room.

"What is this place?"

"It's where people transition from Building 40 to the real world." He shrugs. "It's not so bad. As long as I tell my counselor where I'm going, I can leave the grounds. We have an activity room. We can cook. I'm even taking typing classes."

"The letters, the law firm. Are you really related to him?"

"Who, the Sailor? Of course not. But I figured, no one else was claiming his stuff. I would have acted sooner, but I've been committed since '67. I only moved here in July." He laughs again. "I should have taken the painting that night but, as you know, there were complications."

"You mean the night he died? You were there?"

Steensma nods.

"So were you, it was quite a party. Sarah was going to be the night's entertainment but, for some reason, that left a bad taste in your mouth and you put a stop to things. Not that it'd ever bothered you before." He turns and adds, "Or don't you remember 'Sally Mae'?"

"How do you know all this?"

"I told you, Lou, I'm a big fan. I've been following you for years." Steensma waves his arm at all the clippings and news stories. "I've liked you ever since we met."

"And where was that?"

"You don't remember?"

Lou shakes his head.

"Here, Lou. Creedmoor, back in '59. Our sessions overlapped that summer. That may have been your first round of shock treatments, but I'd been a regular customer for years." He pauses to show Lou the insides of his arms. Scars, about three inches long, run up and down each wrist. "And even though I almost forgot my own name a dozen times, somehow I remembered yours. And when I started seeing your picture in the paper, because of all that crazy stuff with Andy Warhol, it came back to me. That college kid from Long Island I used to talk to at Creedmoor."

"What did I have to do with anything?"

"Well, at first my plan was to go down to the Factory and tell people I knew you. I had enough facts about your life that I felt I could pull it off. Pretending to be your friend, I mean." He stops and gives a big smile. "But none of that was necessary. They saw how crazy I was and let me right in."

"You hung around the Factory? Did you see the band there?"

"Sure. We even had a few conversations. You didn't remember me, of course, and I wasn't eager to advertise my past. Andy might have been fine with people *acting* crazy, but if he knew about Creedmoor, I would have been kicked out for sure."

"And then you met the Sailor?"

"And then we *all* met the Sailor, Lou. For a while he was the only thing anyone talked about. Until he went too far."

"The film," Lou says.

"You know about the Sailor's little home movie? I was hoping to be the star, to be put out of my misery once and for all, but he picked somebody else."

"Who was she?"

"That little waif he strangled? Oh, just some bored girl from the suburbs who came to the city looking for excitement. The streets were filled with them back then." He turns and looks out the window. "Probably still are."

Lou sits down on the bed, trying to process everything he's hearing.

"Is that why you did it, Lou? Kill him, I mean. Did *you* want the girl? She didn't seem your type, maybe because she was a female."

"Donato?" Lou looks up. "I didn't kill him."

Steensma laughs.

"Oh, yes you did. I saw you do it. Sarah saw it. Even Andy saw it."

Lou stands up quickly.

"Warhol was there?"

"Andy had met the Sailor at the Factory a bunch of times, but he'd never actually seen him do his thing in person. That night was meant to be a sort of command performance. Until you went and ruined everything."

Lou tries to clear the clouds in his brain.

"I didn't kill him," he repeats.

Steensma grins.

"Oh, yes you did. And I can prove it."

"How?"

"Your song, Lou. 'Sister Ray.'" He reaches down and pulls out a copy of *White Light/White Heat*. Lou can faintly see the skull tattoo in the half-light of the room. "It's all there."

"I made that up," Lou protests, "it's just a story. About drag queens."

"You changed some *details*, sure, but it'll still be enough for a jury. Hell, your reputation alone will put you behind bars."

As Steensma puts down the album, Lou grabs the suitcase and places it on the bed. He pulls out Donato's address book.

"Your name's Tim, right? If you're in this book, it'll prove you knew him. I'll find out where you were. What you were doing back then."

As Lou talks, Steensma examines the contents of the suitcase. The gun wrapped in the T-shirt is sitting atop the film can, the wooden handle peeking out from cotton swaddling. He grabs the revolver.

"This is the gun," Steensma says slowly, "from that night. I recognize it."

Lou steps away, backing into the radiator.

Steensma slowly raises his arm and points the revolver at Lou's head.

"It's time for you to pay for what you did."

"I'm telling you, I didn't kill him."

"Lou, just because you don't remember doesn't mean you didn't do it." The gun in Steensma's hand begins to shake. "And this way it all works out. You get what's coming to you, and I get the painting."

Lou lunges forward, knocking the gun loose. It lands on the dresser and crashes into the row of pills. Two of the bottles shower their contents all over the desk and floor.

The two men fall first to the bed and then onto the rug. Searching blindly under the desk with a free hand, Lou feels the coldness of the gun. He grabs it, pushes away Steensma, and scrambles to stand up. As soon as Lou gets to his feet, Steensma hits him across the face, sending him backward. The gun flies out of his hand. Lou crashes against the window as Steensma scoops up the gun from the floor. Before he can take aim, Lou leaps upon Steensma. Lou feels the gun go against his ribs and then his gut. He searches frantically with his hands until they find the revolver. When he finds it, he pulls the trigger.

The sound's muffled since the gun is pressed directly against Steensma's chest. The sound of skin, blood, and bone splattering against the wall makes more of a noise than the muted firing of the pistol. Steensma bucks once and becomes dead weight, falling against Lou. Lou gets out of the way and lets the body fall to the floor. The air smells like spent gunpowder.

While Steensma bleeds out onto the carpet, Lou quickly grabs from the walls all the articles about Warhol and the Velvet Underground. He throws them into the suitcase, tosses in the gun, and closes it. He grabs the suitcase and leaves the room.

Even though the hallway is empty, Lou hears voices.

He retraces his steps from before, racing quickly down the hallway, the staircase, and out to the sidewalk.

Staring straight ahead, he walks through the streets and around the various buildings, making his way back to the main road. As he watches the cars going by, he wished Ray would have stuck around. Lou needs a ride into Manhattan.

●

It's almost noon by the time he arrives at Union Square. After hailing a cab outside Creedmoor to get to the LIRR in Bellerose, he decided to splurge and get another taxi once he'd arrived in the city, taking him from Penn Station to the Factory. This left only a few dollars in his wallet. To get home he'll have to take the subway.

Switching the suitcase from his right hand to his left, he enters the building and then the elevator. On the sixth floor, the door to the Factory is partly open and Lou can hear voices. The front reception room is empty. Flashes are going off back in the studio. Lou walks further, quietly, still holding the suitcase. He finds Fred Hughes and Andy circling a tall woman with high cheekbones, dark-green eyes, and a mane of blond hair. She's wearing a black dress and a necklace made of huge gold rings. Warhol's taking pictures while Fred keeps telling the woman how fabulous she looks.

"Lou."

Warhol notices him and lowers the camera.

"Come, Yoyo, let's go check your makeup." Fred

Hughes leads her toward the front room. "Maybe we can try a few shots with your hair back."

After they leave, Lou asks, "Who's that?"

"Wife of Bruno Bischofberger. They're Swiss, have a gallery in Zurich. *Very* rich." Andy sets the camera down onto a low table that holds three flutes of champagne. "What are you doing here, Lou?"

"Why didn't you tell me about Donato? That you'd been there the night he was killed?"

Andy rolls his eyes.

"You're still thinking about *that*?"

Lou leans in and says in a whisper, "I saw your little film."

"That wasn't one of ours, Lou. Though, the Sailor wanted me to release it. Can you *imagine*? We had a hard-enough time with Viva in Tucson faking getting raped. There would have been a riot if we had shown *Snuff*."

Lou raises the suitcase. "I have a copy of it right here."

Warhol doesn't respond to this. He just looks over the glasses of champagne.

"Andy, why didn't you tell me I was the one who killed him?"

"The Sailor? You didn't kill him, Lou."

"Then who did?"

"Some young guy, I don't know his name. He'd only come around the Factory a few times."

Lou goes to the wall of Polaroids. The rows and rows of faces.

"He and the Sailor had some sort of *disagreement* about something," Warhol continues. "I think it was about the film. He showed up to the party and things went downhill. Everybody went home. What else do you want me to say?"

There, toward the bottom, Lou sees him. Steensma. Lou plucks the photo from the wall.

"Is this him?"

Andy lazily turns his head.

"Yes, Lou, that's him. You know him?"

"I just met him. And I think I just killed him."

Warhol shrugs.

"Then it all worked out."

Conversation and laughter can be heard from the other room.

"You think this is a happy ending, Andy? Three people have been murdered."

"It's New York City, Lou. Those kinds of things happen. That's what makes it New York City." He points to the suitcase. "Will you do me a favor? Get rid of the movie."

"What do you want me to do with it?"

Andy waves his hands in the air.

"I don't know, make it disappear. Change the channel."

Nodding numbly, Lou picks up the suitcase and begins to leave.

"Lou," Warhol calls after him, "write a song about it."

He stops and turns around.

"I think I already did."

In the reception area, Hughes is helping the woman take off a pair of black high heels. He looks just like a shoe salesman. Lou leaves the Factory, slamming the door behind him.

The elevator arrives at the ground floor and Lou walks

out onto the sidewalk. The day's turned cool. The artists and merchants with their displays and tables along the east side of Union Square are wearing jackets and scarves. Lou can see stalls filled with paintings, touristy and cheap, sitting next to guys selling hats and gloves. Fall will be here soon, so people are more interested in the hats and gloves.

Standing on the corner, suitcase in his hand, he waits for the traffic to subside before walking against the light at Fifteenth Street. A taxi honks but he doesn't flinch. He cuts across the southern edge of the park, heading for the subway entrance on Broadway. He passes a few NYU students marching with banners denouncing the war. Lou ignores them and walks slowly down the subway steps, gradually disappearing underground.

9 781733 112864